T0375698

Getting It

Daniel Shaviro

iUniverse, Inc.
New York   Bloomington

Getting It

iUniverse books may be ordered through booksellers or by contacting:

iUniverse
1663 Liberty Drive
Bloomington, IN 47403
www.iuniverse.com
1-800-Authors (1-800-288-4677)

Because of the dynamic nature of the Internet, any Web addresses or
links contained in this book may have changed since publication and
may no longer be valid. The views expressed in this work are solely those
of the author and do not necessarily reflect the views of the publisher,
and the publisher hereby disclaims any responsibility for them.

ISBN: 978-1-4401-9291-3 (pbk)
ISBN: 978-1-4401-9292-0 (ebk)

Printed in the United States of America

iUniverse rev. date: 2/22/2010

1. The Legions of Hate

At the well-appointed offices of Ashby & Cinders, Peter Crossley, the partner who had been rather casually appointed to handle the new Barlow matter, was waiting for his subordinates. They were due to visit him at 4 o'clock, and already it was 3:59:30.

Crossley had the etiquette of the situation firmly in hand. For the associates to arrive early would be unexampled cheek - as if he weren't busy every moment of the day prior to the appointment. To arrive late would be unexampled cheek - as if he could wait all day for them, when his time was worth $250 per hour.

Fortunately, Crossley had ordered his secretary not to admit them until precisely 4:05. And at 4:04:45, he could place a call to his wife. This way, after their five minute wait outside, he could make them wait in his office for another ten minutes, staring if they liked at the contrast between the light gray carpet and dark gray chairs, and feeling uncomfortable while he engaged in personal conversation. With any luck, they would rise apologetically to leave, and he would be able to wave them impatiently back into their chairs.

Crossley licked his thin, bloodless lips as he reviewed the situation. Assignment to the Barlow case was a dubious honor; it was unlikely to generate much in the way of either billings or glory. Had he been assigned to it out of contempt - the why-waste-our-best philosophy? Or to make him look bad? Or simply by lot, because someone senior thought it was his turn? On the other hand, it was nicely timed to let him enjoy flexing his already well-honed metaphorical muscles. With a little crude hinting, he could imply to the associates, without being far wrong, that the case was a life-or-death affair - the last crucial step, taken under his watchful eye, in determining which, if any, of them would make partner.

Crossley could easily visualize the pleasures that awaited him. First, in six weeks, would come the annual partners' meeting. There would be the flattering attention as he gave his precis of each associate. The faint praise he would offer - compliments for one's energy, another's thoroughness, a third's nuts and bolts knowhow. The expression of concern - the problems that worried Crossley about each one's performance. Much as he liked his proteges, he would say, it was his duty to share these concerns. Finally, there would be the exquisite agony of telling probably two, but better yet all three, of the associates that they would be well advised to seek employment elsewhere. As the type of person who had tortured insects as a boy but since fallen victim to a tender conscience, Crossley rarely felt pleasures as delicious as at that horrible moment when an associate's eyes would pop open upon grasping the bad news.

By now, it was 4:05 and, though he had not placed his phone call, two of the associates were admitted. Their order of entry had all the inevitability, if none of the tragedy, of Greek tragedy. First was eager Bill Doberman, loudly saluting him and claiming to have left Mr. Cinders "in the lurch" in order to arrive in time for the meeting. Doberman was immediately followed by Lowell Stellworth, the languid yet fanatical master of the lengthy footnote. Only Arnold Porter had not arrived. This poor soul, painfully earnest and perennially besieged, could be expected late as usual, puffing his apologies about being detained by another partner.

Doberman and Stellworth made a kind of Jeff and Jeff pair as they entered without Porter, the Mutt of the group. Each was a smidgen under six feet, and convinced that he was slightly the taller of the two.

They were so poorly matched, however, that any good interior decorator would have applauded Crossley's plan to trade in at least one of them next month. Doberman was trim, with smooth skin, symmetrical features, and white teeth that he flashed a lot (whether to smile or grimace) because he knew from looking at the bathroom mirror that they were striking. The secretaries admired his cheekbones, and the contrast between his healthy pink skin and almost black hair. His eyes were also dark, although perhaps a bit too big and staring - the main criticism one heard in the hallways - but some found this intense and magnetic. He was prone to make direct eye contact to the point of being invasive, evidently relishing this as an assertion of will.

Stellworth was long-limbed and gangly, with pale blond hair that he combed straight back, leaving a large forehead over his brown wire-rim glasses. The secretaries applauded his upright posture and old-money air, but found his body movements awkward. They also noted that his eyes were not quite even and his teeth oddly spaced and a bit yellow. Perhaps he should have used the braces that his dentist must have suggested long ago.

Their mode of dress was almost a match. Both had chosen medium gray suits today; and for both it was usually either that, or charcoal, or light gray with pinstripes (they happened to have pinstriped the same color tone), or else dark blue. Doberman, today and especially in the charcoal, favored a tighter, more Italian rather than Brooks Brothers cut. He had also jumped with both feet onto the yellow tie bandwagon, and today was wearing a specimen that Stellworth, who favored dark red with understated stripes or dots, would have gone so far – although he knew this was bordering on the unfair – as to call garish.

"I can never get over what a nice office you have!" Doberman exclaimed as he darted over the threshold and paused, leaving no more room for Stellworth than was strictly necessary. Stellworth winced as he squeezed through; his own methods of sycophancy were less direct.

"I like it," responded Crossley, flashing the ghastly forced smile with which he always expected, quite misguidedly, to reassure his interlocutors. "I always say that, from my double window, it almost looks like Paris, more than Washington. All those broad boulevards and sidewalk cafes."

"Not just that! It's so spacious, and you've furnished it with such excellent taste. If I had this office, I wouldn't change a thing."

This was almost going too far. Doberman was ambitious enough to want the office himself, although there was no conceivable way he would ever get it. Even Crossley, a partner for eight years, had been lucky when a senior partner retired and everyone above him in the pecking order was too busy or preoccupied to move. If Crossley had his way, and assuming the accuracy of the office hours he claimed to keep, there was about a 40 percent chance that he would die here.

Porter shambled in, precariously balancing a stack of law books. He was about five foot eight, with rounded shoulders, unruly brown hair, heavy eyebrows, and a face that was puffy from interrupted sleep. Evidently his boys had gotten him up again. Most of the secretaries forgave his presentational failings, such as the spots on his pants and ties, on the ground that his bashfulness was endearing. Even so, they were glad that his wife had made him shed his black-framed glasses -

standard Hollywood issue to telegraph the "nerd" character in a group - in favor of hard contact lenses.

Crossley, to paper over any tension about the late arrival, grinned again and asked the associates if they would like his secretary to bring them coffee. All assented - Doberman, to show his fervent approval of every Crossley suggestion; Stellworth, because he had not touched coffee for nearly twenty minutes; and Porter, because he was afraid to say no.

Crossley cleared his throat and ran a hand through his sandy, thinning hair. He tried to pull in his paunch, a recent and distressing addition to his body frame that made him resent these barely more than thirty-year-old associates all the more.

"I hope none of you has irrevocable plans for the weekend. A rather urgent situation has arisen." He paused significantly, and Stellworth shot a prying look at Doberman, hoping to catch an indiscreet flicker of disappointment.

"You are probably aware that we represent Barlow Industries, the tobacco, chemical, and oil drilling company. Until now, we have only handled their tax work and acquisitions. But now they may want us to take over an ongoing administrative proceeding."

Doberman warmly congratulated him, as if on a personal achievement. Stellworth tried to look as if it was only to be expected, and Porter issued a grunt of uncertain meaning.

"It's a very sympathetic case. About ten years ago – well, 1974, so nine years ago – Barlow started selling cigarettes with a new chemical. It was supposed to make them cheaper to produce, yet, according to the surveys, better tasting. They haven't used the chemical for at least four years. But now the FPHC wants to establish a trust fund for supposed tort claims of the federal and state governments and Barlow's customers, by fining Barlow more than three hundred million dollars."

Porter was public-spirited, or foolish, enough to ask what "FPHC" stood for.

Daniel Shaviro

"Federal Public Health Commission. A new agency, created last year in a rider to a water projects bill, so the President couldn't veto it." Crossley frowned at this trick, as disapprovingly as he would have smiled approvingly had Ashby & Cinders been the responsible lobbyist. He was hoping to break into lobbying work more; his wife had Democratic Party connections and perhaps it could even lead to an agency or White House position someday. Crossley, as a rare Washington native and one who had stayed home even for college and law school, knew that while everyone in town was a lawyer - at least it seemed that way - lawyers had only intermediate status if they actually practiced law. Better far to be a lawyer cum fixer in the Executive Branch, or cum power behind the scenes at some key House committee (in the Senate you had to worry about shifting majorities), or at the very least a self-appointed expert on weapons systems or international relations. The Barlow case seemed unlikely to help with any of that.

"It turns out that the Commissioners are so averse to the work they were appointed to do that they've delegated all of their fact-finding to a bunch of staffers. A disaster. These staffers are loose wheels from the civil service who take their marching orders from government scientists and are completely lacking in political sensitivity."

Porter shifted in his seat and Crossley looked down at them again.

Again Porter voiced a thought common to all three associates, but that the other two would not have mentioned even under the bastinado, a medieval Turkish torture involving beating on the soles of the feet with a stick or cudgel, or the strappado, a contemporaneous Italian specialty whereby the victim was lifted by the back, using a pulley, and then dropped halfway.

"Are those the cigarettes we've been reading about in the papers?"

Crossley winced at the tactlessness of this question. He

could not be angry, or at least angrier than he was at humanity generally. Porter was innocent enough to ask this without intending a nasty insinuation.

"They are and they aren't. If everything the newspapers said was true," - but here he faltered, unable to think of a punch line.

"Anyway, the reporting has been quite inaccurate. No one died from the chemical unless there were other complications. The allegations that it tripled cancer risks are unsubstantiated. The same applies to those wild charges about highs and addiction.

"Just to give you an idea of how careless and irresponsible the newspapers have been, I have an article here that misspells the name of the Chief Counsel of the FPHC. The same article alleges that the chemical (TDC, you know, at least they got that right) was first discovered twelve years ago, in 1971, whereas the actual date was 1969.

"But it seems that all the Commissioners care about is politics. They're so desperate to make the six o'clock news that they've recently issued an order locking up enough of Barlow's assets to guarantee payment of a fine in the worst-case scenario. Talk about kicking a company when it's down ten percent in the stock market! We only have until Monday to write a brief showing that the government's chance of prevailing is too low for the order to stay in force pending final resolution."

"Isn't that rather short notice?" asked Doberman. "I'd be happy to do it, of course."

"The case has been going on for some time. Only the order to seize assets at this stage in the proceedings is new. Barlow was so upset that they were on the verge of firing Nesson & Wesson, their counsel up to now, and substituting us. The brief is due on Wednesday but if we get it to them by the close of business on Monday they'll decide which brief they like better: ours or the other guy's.

"It's a bit of a long shot for us at this point, but the thing might have legs. Reply brief in six weeks, final agency decision maybe in a year, then of course Barlow will head to federal court if they aren't satisfied."

Too bad I'm positioned to take the blame for such a long shot at leveraging into all of that upside, Crossley thought. Not that I'll stand alone in the dock with the partnership meeting and senior associate review coming up so soon. I've got more suspects right in front of me here than I could shake a stick at using both arms. I mean, even giving each arm its own stick.

Doberman, meanwhile, was wondering if he looked bad for not knowing about the FPHC inquiry. On the one hand, it might suggest that he was not carefully reading the Wall Street Journal that the firm supplied to all its lawyers. On the other hand, perhaps there was nothing wrong with being too busy to follow current events.

"Is there any chance of an extension?" he asked. "I'm just concerned about the firm's reputation for quality. We can get you an excellent product by Monday, but I know how you like to massage a brief, and get it just right."

"Quality is exactly what I'm concerned about," Crossley responded. "Do you realize that no one has even found a typo in an Ashby & Cinders product for over four years?" It was hard not to realize this; Mr. Ashby had mentioned it at the last three monthly firm lunches. And this was before the invention of Spellcheck.

"But as for the extension, I'm afraid it's impossible. We, or rather previous counsel, have already exceeded the limit for requesting delay, and Barlow was told, fortunately after they decided to get us involved, that at this stage even new counsel wouldn't do it.

"At any rate, it is now Friday afternoon. I need a completed brief on my desk by 9 o'clock on Monday morning. That way I'll have time to look it over carefully before getting it to the client's Washington office by 5 o'clock. No late submissions, please. I really should ask for it by Sunday night."

Crossley was relieved to see that the preliminaries had passed without rebellion. In particular, no one had asked the awkward question of why he had waited until 4 o'clock to tell them. He turned the conversation to the details of the Monday submission.

"There are three topics that we need to brief. First, the scientific facts and evidence. At this stage, it obviously is not feasible to master them completely. But we must be able to summarize all the main points from the hearings, and show that we're in good shape on the facts."

"Second, there is the issue of jurisdiction. At least for the future, the FPHC has the power to enforce the law they're acting under. But these alleged wrongs occurred before they even existed. We think that only the agencies that existed at the time can act now. Obviously, the FPHC enforcement arm disagrees.

"Finally, there is the issue of assumption of risk. This is my favorite argument. The Surgeon General already warns cigarette smokers about the dangers of smoking - what more do they want?" And he chuckled at the thought that this mandated warning, so deeply offensive to all right-thinking counsel of tobacco companies, might prove to have some value after all.

"Can we get any help?" asked Doberman. "Aside from extra secretaries, I mean."

Crossley knew that Doberman was thirsting to ride herd over the junior associates, but decided to give the question a more limited interpretation.

"Until Monday, you're on your own. After that, I'm sure we can spare a paralegal to help with the scientific evidence. We might need that for the reply brief if we get lucky."

It was at this point that Stellworth, previously silent in his intensely contemplative manner, decided to launch a daring gambit.

"What about Lyla Stamper?" he asked. "From what I hear,

she's always given satisfaction." And he glanced at Doberman with equal elements of defiance and distaste.

Doberman immediately understood both the brilliance and the deceptive subtlety of this gambit. Indeed, as a fellow master at infighting, he could not help admiring it. Wellington reacted similarly upon learning of Napoleon's lightning return from Elba. So did Bugs Bunny when Daffy told Elmer it was rabbit season.

Superficially, Stellworth was sneering at Doberman's semi-known affair with Stamper. He meant to imply both that it violated office rules of rank and decorum, and that it showed an essential frivolity, as if man could not live by work alone. No more direct attack was possible, since the Doberman-Stamper entanglement was semi-officially off the record.

On a deeper level, however, known only to Stellworth and Doberman, Stellworth was maneuvering for all-important position in the ongoing partnership war between the three associates. Crossley had already stated that his favorite topic was assumption of risk. By contrast, the scientific evidence could be a perilous sand pit, particularly since it had to be summarized accurately by Monday. By bringing Stamper into the case, Stellworth obviously hoped to lure Doberman into this pit, thus eliminating a key rival in the jousting for assumption of risk. Stellworth had heard rumors that Doberman and Stamper were having problems, and Doberman might well think that working with her would help repair the bond. If so, Doberman might rationalize to himself that the scientific evidence was a big enough challenge to bring the biggest potential payoff. Not true, of course - the partners gave demerits for mistakes much more readily than credit for extraordinary achievement.

"Fine with me," said Doberman calmly, addressing himself to Crossley. "And why not let us carve up the topics among ourselves?"

Crossley nodded, his eagerness to abate the human presence in his office for once overriding his lust for control. He knew the associates would care about who got what, but did not feel like siding with one of them against the others right now. Let them carry on like scorpions in a bottle with a juicy caterpillar and, if they had to come back to him for a resolution, then he could add a three-way demerit on partnership night: Lack of Teamwork.

"Just one more thing, then," he said, pressing his hands together and sitting upright. "I don't have to tell you about the importance of your performance here." So he didn't. But for the next five and a quarter seconds, Crossley stared at the three associates in turn, his meaning so clear that, while he uttered not a word, any one of them could have transcribed and attributed to him the following implicit speech:

"As you all know, you are sixth-year associates. The next formal review will decide everything. Now, we can't make everyone partner, much as we'd like to; this is still a business, not a charity.

"I will be watching you very closely in this head-to-head test. I want to give you all very fair, and if possible favorable, assessments to the full partnership concerning which of you I think - if any - is partnership material."

"So act accordingly!!!"

These words, although unspoken, had their effect. The room began, even more than previously, to seethe with hatred. Crossley hated everyone there, including himself. Doberman and Stellworth each hated everyone except himself. Porter hated himself.

Crossley's intercom buzzer sounded. Picking it up, and hearing that Cinders was calling, he switched to the indicated phone line and crooned a soft greeting, in keeping with his aim to be a consummate TATB man (toady above, tyrannize below). Suddenly he blinked his eyes in pain and covered the mouthpiece with his hand.

"I think that's all. Doberman, Cinders wants to see you in his office. He says it's not business."

2. The Eastern Front

As the three associates trooped out of Crossley's office, Doberman, in front as usual, turned his head and suggested that they meet "ASAP."

"Of course," he added, "I'm not sure exactly when I'll be free. Sometimes Cinders just keeps me there forever."

"It won't be long, I'm sure," said Stellworth grimly.

Stellworth's wounds on hearing that Cinders wanted to see Doberman, and not about business, were, if anything, even deeper than Crossley's. While Crossley's chagrin merely expressed his vanity and reflexive self-measurement in terms of his superiors, Stellworth had a more practical motive as well.

Never mind that work, for a man of Stellworth's stamp, was so desperately important as to dwarf all comparatively trivial concerns, such as his family or physical health. It still was by no means the only thing he lived for. Indeed, he viewed the theory that partnership could be attained through work alone much as a Jesuit would contemplate the heresy that salvation can be attained through works alone, without faith. Stellworth was always anxious to prove his absolute fidelity to the ideals that he saw as informing the spirit of Ashby & Cinders.

Thus, what some saw as shameless toadying, Stellworth viewed as a quest for spiritual perfection, both real and manifest. Unfortunately, this quest frequently placed him in direct competition with Doberman, whose appreciation of the requirements for partnership was no less keen. The dream of Stellworth's life, short of partnership itself, was to expose the fraud and hypocrisy in Doberman's artistic rendering of the Ashby & Cinders ideal.

At the moment, if the Barlow case was the newly opened Western front of the Doberman-Stellworth conflict, then the competition for the eye of Mr. Cinders was the Eastern front. Both Doberman and Stellworth wanted to emerge as the premier "nice young fellow" whom Cinders would take on his rounds of hobnobbing with the cream of the corporatocracy - all potential clients - at museum board meetings and charitable events. To this end, the two associates continually were trying to out-culture each other.

For neither did this role come entirely naturally. Doberman, plotting a course for law school since the age of sixteen, had not, until his arrival at Ashby & Cinders, realized the diversity of the relevant qualifications, not just for partnership but beyond. Stellworth had grown up with the sense that art appreciation was like church services. You were supposed to go through the motions, but without undue enthusiasm. Why had nobody warned him that the arts, unlike religion, would ultimately require glib speech and the exercise of judgment?

No historian is likely to reconstruct the earlier history of the deadly struggle, but its warp and woof lingered in the memories of the participants. There had been l'Affaire Chateauneuf - the miraculous "vin trouvé," boasted of by Doberman, that Stellworth insisted sounded more like a Cabernet. There had been harsh disagreements about the singers at a Washington Opera performance of *Madame*

Butterfly. In the realm of painting, where both were anxious to play it safe by their respective lights, there had been disputes about the supremacy of Rembrandt (Stellworth's idol) or the Impressionists (endorsed by Doberman).

Now Doberman hoped, and Stellworth feared, that Cinders' summons betokened a decisive stage in the conflict. It is well-known that trivial events can have momentous consequences - even if the rumors that one hears about straws and camels' backs are rumors only. Thus, Doberman wondered if his recent offhand comment that "The second time you look, of course, Monet is so much better than Manet" – or had he put it the other way around? - might have succeeded beyond all expectations.

With this hope, Doberman almost bounced into Cinders' office, a merry phrase of greeting on his lips. Immediately he had to choke it back. Cinders was on the phone.

The seconds passed into minutes. Doberman looked around him at an office that, unlike Crossley's, seemed far beyond aspiration. The size of eight associates' offices or maybe three ordinary partners', it departed from the decorating scheme of all other Ashby & Cinders office space. Elsewhere the main colors were contrasting grays, with wall-to-wall carpeting, bright white paint on the walls, black-lettered name plates, and, as a kind of Vincent Price touch to offset the general austerity, dark maroon cubicles for the secretaries in the hallways. Cinders' office featured cherry hardwood floors set off by orange and brown area kilims, next to light pastel walls (yellow here and green there) holding four good-sized paintings: one Chagall print, two Abstract Expressionist, and an Impressionist-influenced contemporary rendering of a covered bridge in winter. The last of these paintings, Cinders liked to mention, he had personally commissioned from a moderately well-known New York artist, a Hans Hoffman student whose country place was near his own in Maine.

The white-maned, bow-tied, Roman-nosed Cinders was

evidently indifferent to Doberman's presence, or at least skilled in conveying that impression; there were none of the sidelong glances by which Crossley would betray his pleasure in making people wait. Finally Doberman caught Cinders' attention, but Cinders only rolled his eyes towards the door, silently mouthing the words "I'll call you," and Doberman was forced to retreat.

There was no time for Doberman to pause and lick his wounds. Knowing that Stellworth would be spying in the coffee room nearby in any case, he resolved to bring the Barlow meeting to order immediately. He called Porter from the secretary's desk, scheduled the meeting for his own office, and then found Stellworth by the coffee machine.

Stellworth raised an eyebrow upon hearing of the scheduled location. "Why not use a conference room?" he asked. "There's one right by my office."

"I thought you'd be more comfortable on my sofa."

This stung; Stellworth's office did not have a sofa, or even a boxy, law school dorm era, off-white love seat from home with a barely discernible stain on the left arm, which was all that Doberman really had. So, changing his tactics, Stellworth sighed heavily and asked about the meeting with Cinders.

"Oh, just a little something that he wanted to ask me about," said Doberman in his most offhand manner. "He'll be calling to consult me further in a few minutes."

"He was too busy to talk to you."

Doberman raised his eyebrows noncommittally. The two were silent for the duration of the walk to Doberman's office, each marshaling his strength for the battle that lay ahead. They found Porter waiting for them outside the door. Somehow, he managed only to be late for meetings with partners.

As Doberman settled into the dark gray swivel chair behind his desk, he felt relaxed and buoyant. The other two looked so like associates as they leaned forward on the love seat. They had to look up at him, their pads on their knees, while he could rock back in his chair and contemplate the ceiling.

Even better, Doberman was a step ahead of Stellworth in his grasp of the situation. Stellworth might be expecting the Lyla Stamper gambit to have weakened Doberman's resolve to demand assumption of risk, but in fact it had only brought out his fighting blood. And an off-balance, over-confident Stellworth would have little chance against a lean, hard, hungry Doberman.

But then, just as Doberman was preparing his opening remarks, full of gracious reassurance about his willingness to take assumption of risk off everyone's hands, a startling thing happened. Porter, usually the meekest of men, launched an unanticipated salvo.

"I'm sure that you both want assumption of risk, and don't want to let the other one do it. So why not compromise? Let me do it."

There was a dead silence from the other two.

"I don't think I'm being unduly pushy. It's not like I always get my way."

Doberman felt like a boxer who, while glaring at his opponent during the referee's instructions, is suddenly stung on the back of the head by a giant hornet. Lee Marvin had a similar experience, in *The Man Who Shot Liberty Valance*, when he was shot from behind while steadying his aim to plug Jimmy Stewart right between the eyes.

Stellworth hardly felt better. This showed how right he was to tattle whenever Porter's childcare arrangements broke down and he had to leave the office early for a pick-up. On second thought, however, Stellworth found Porter's suggestion intriguing. Perhaps it would be rash to hazard open warfare over assumption of risk. Since Porter could not be regarded as a serious threat, at least assumption of risk would be neutralized as a source of danger. It also might be easier to steer Doberman towards the scientific evidence once the most glamorous alternative was out of the picture. And it would not be terribly surprising if Doberman made some ghastly blunder about the evidence - sometimes he lacked Stellworth's patience and attention to detail.

Stellworth accordingly produced a sickly grin and mumbled his agreement. "As for me," he continued, "I'd be happy to write up the jurisdictional issue. I've researched the subject before and have several memos in my files."

Doberman stared at the two of them. "Are you sure that's the best arrangement for the firm? Remember that we want to do the best job possible.

"I would be happy to handle the scientific evidence if only I were convinced that was the best allocation of my abilities. But I'm not at my best, and I know it's a weakness, on subjects that don't involve either intellectual creativity or hardnosed legal research. Anyway, I've had some ideas about assumption of risk that I'd hate to see wasted."

"Like what?" asked Porter.

Doberman was forced to improvise. "I anticipate a, how shall I put it, a chiaroscuro approach. Light and shadow, you know, like Italian painting. Highlight the strong points, and hide the ball on the others."

"What strong and weak points?" Stellworth demanded. "Crossley didn't say anything about them."

"I'd hate to summarize them here. They need a bit more polish. Anyway, I don't want to prove too much." Doberman didn't know what this meant, but had always liked its sound.

At this juncture, Doberman again experienced something more common in boxing than in the legal world - the sensation of reeling on the ropes and being saved by the bell. First his phone rang, and then the buzzer for his private intercom.

He picked up the intercom, listened for a second, and then broke into a broad grin. "You'll have to pipe down for a minute," he told the other associates. "Cinders is calling."

"Yes," he said into the phone, "I'd be happy to talk to him.

"Hello? Mr. Cinders?" he faltered. There was a pause. Then Doberman started nodding vigorously, even though his interlocutor obviously could not see him. He started to speak, loudly enough for the convenience of Stellworth and Porter.

"Yes... I see your point... That's simply fascinating…

"You mean that little comment I made about Monet versus Manet?. . .His portraiture ... Not so much the brushwork as the lines... Well yes, I take your point …

"What an excellent idea! I'd love to take a look at it... No, I was thinking maybe next week....

"You mean Sunday's the last day? The gallery is starting a new exhibition? In that case, I'm not sure I should...

"Other obligations. Big brief coming down...

"Oh, I know. You've told me that a thousand times. It's just that I told Stellworth and Porter here that I'd take the most difficult part... Oh, scientific evidence. I have to master and summarize it by Monday. Completely, you know. Up to our usual standards...

"No, we haven't started working on it yet... Why, yes, there is another topic I could do a good job on and still have time for the exhibit...

"Assumption of risk... I was thinking I would try a chiaroscuro effect." He laughed. "I guess you could say that...

"Very good. I'll let everyone know your preference...No, thank *you*. Goodbye."

Doberman replaced the phone receiver and glanced down at Stellworth and Porter. "There you have it. He simply insisted. Lowell, you can still do jurisdiction, and Arnold, why don't you try the scientific evidence?"

The two glumly left his office. Once they were safely gone, Doberman broke into a jubilant smile and pumped his fist in the air. Cinders had received another call while his secretary was dialing Doberman. After the first ten seconds, Doberman had been speaking into a dead phone line.

3. A Dilemma

Doberman was still savoring this triumph when the phone rang again. To his disappointment, however, it was Lyla Stamper, rather than Cinders calling back.

"Are you ready to leave yet?" she asked him.

Suddenly he remembered that they had been scheduled to have dinner with her mother Doris. He had not been looking forward to it.

Doberman lived a sufficiently dashing private life to have dined with quite a few girlfriends' parents. Of these, Doris definitely was not the worst. That honor went to the mother who seemed to have a little Doberman doll on her bedroom dresser. So far so good; only, it was a voodoo object with pins stuck through it.

Though not quite in this class, Doris shared the popular parental view of Doberman as potentially an excellent catch but untrustworthy and likely to prove a cad. On the last occasion when they had dined with Doris, she had snorted loudly when the subject of air pollution came up. To her, pollution meant only one thing: what Doberman was doing to her daughter.

So it was with some complacency that Doberman informed Lyla that work pressures would prevent his going to dinner.

"What about tomorrow night?" she asked.

"I just can't do it."

There was an ominous silence, and Doberman knew he was on dangerous ground. Lyla was both close to and sensitive about her mother. They lived together, although she could have afforded her own place. A nasty divorce from the father when Lyla was eleven had cemented a powerful and in some ways (until Doberman) even exclusive alliance between the two of them. Lyla had only recently agreed to meet with the father, who remained unmentionable in polite company for his infidelities and desertion. Her siblings, a girl three years older and a boy three years younger, had each in different ways been the wrong age to become Mother's choice companion when the disaster struck, and by now they had long since left the field.

Doberman well remembered the painful occasion on which he had made a tactless reference to the old lady upon seeing a medieval battle-axe at the Smithsonian. Yet the appearance of snubbing Doris was only one of the dangers that he needed to avoid. There also was the problem of Lyla's acute jealousy. Although he discouraged overtly discussing fidelity or even their future together, she exacted punishment whenever she suspected him of straying in thought or deed.

Doberman enjoyed his relationship with Lyla, whom he considered the very apotheosis of the health spa. She was all straight lines, perennially crisp and presentable with her slim build and athletic, almost tomboyish, figure. Her dark brown hair, kept short and straight in a pageboy cut, was always in place, unless he tousled it while they were alone and earned squeals of protest. Her eyes were green and set far apart, above a fine straight nose and thin but wide lips. At the office she usually wore white shirts, turned up at the elbows in nice weather, and paired with knee-length skirts in somber patterns or dark solids. Only Doberman knew about her teddy collection, partly bought by him, and the rest by her to please him.

Sometimes Lyla would ask if he thought her breasts were too small, but he would say: Don't you realize that Rubensesque means fat? There also were bonds between them beyond the physical. They squabbled frequently, but this was not really a minus. Doberman admired her strong will, the more so because he wanted to subjugate her. Their intimate, competitive struggle reminded him of his pre-lone wolf days, growing up in Connecticut with his brother. Patrick Doberman, just fourteen months older than Bill but always markedly taller and heavier, had played Lennon to Bill's McCartney throughout their childhood together. Then in the early 1970s he had dropped out of college and disappeared for a while, evidently losing a few years to drugs, and finally re-emerging as an overweight high school English teacher back in Hartford where they had grown up. Loser, Doberman thought, and they were no longer close (he rarely went home anyway). But perhaps Lyla had taken the Patrick slot from his childhood, or really the Bill slot since she was the junior companion. Maybe this was why sometimes it seemed as if half the fun of his law firm intrigues - well, okay, maybe more like a quarter or a fifth, but still that was significant - came from the knowledge that he would shortly be able to dramatize to Lyla what he was up to, naturally not without embroidering it a bit.

This much Lyla might perhaps have guessed about his sense of the relationship, although they liked to live in the present rather than ruminate about how they had gotten here. She was not, however, aware of an underlying Doberman calculation. He had learned that her mysterious and absconded father still lived in Washington, and indeed was the last-named partner at Carp, Stone & Tyler, a moderately respectable Washington law firm. (Stamper was her mother's maiden name.) Admittedly, the firm was not as prestigious as Ashby & Cinders. Still, Doberman thought of Lyla as his fallback position. If he did not make partner here, he could marry her and reasonably expect an offer from the father's firm to follow. Surely the dad owed her that much in return for the occasional dinner dates that she had only recently agreed to (not that he was pressing for any more than that). And besides, Carp, Stone & Tyler would be lucky to get a Doberman, even one who was temporarily bearing the stench of what remained at this point a totally hypothetical partnership rejection. Surely Lyla would be willing to take a deep breath and ask Dad for help on Doberman's behalf if things ever came to that.

To ease the tension with Lyla about canceling dinner, Doberman began describing the Barlow case, along with a discreetly sanitized version of the intrigues over assumption of risk. This was always a good way to handle her. Much of his appeal to her arose from his aura of power and success, which fed her fantasies of a glamorous, ruthless couple rising to the top of the Washington social ladder.

"I wish there was some way I could see you," he concluded. "I wish I could spend the whole weekend with you. But it's simply impossible, even for a couple of hours. I may have to put in 40 hours by Monday morning. You know how high a standard they have here, and how they expect everything to be letter perfect. Crossley will be running his eagle eye over it, just praying for some mistake that he can use against me to pay me back for getting a call from Cinders."

"But you always say that the least important thing is what goes on between the white lines."

"Not in a case as big as this. Even if I snow Crossley, there's Nesson & Wesson to think about. They'd love to show Barlow our screw-up to help them keep the case."

Doberman summoned himself for a further effort. The love-word would evidently have to be mentioned, and so it was.

Lyla was mollified, if not very pleased. Doberman was considering whether flowers - better yet, for Doris - would be overdoing it when his phone rang again. Cinders, in person rather than through a secretary as usual, was on the line.

"Hello? Hello?" Cinders burbled.

"Mr. Cinders! I was just about to call you!"

"Bill, I was wondering if you could help me with something."

Since they were not face to face, Doberman did not bother to salute.

"You know my love for the opera. I have subscription tickets for this Sunday. Wagner's *Meistersinger*. My wife and I have been looking forward to it."

Doberman vented thrilled congratulations.

"Unfortunately, some in-laws have arrived and we cannot go."

"Have you thought about selling the tickets?" Doberman asked, not wanting to be presumptuous.

Cinders briefly considered charging Doberman for them, but decided against it. "No. I remembered how much you like opera."

Doberman was speechless. To think that Cinders remembered or cared enough to have chosen him - this was real progress! But the tragedy of it was that he faced forty or more hours of assumption of risk. Nor could he use the opera just as a short break. Wagner operas were reputed to last longer than the careers of some Ashby & Cinders associates.

"I adore it," he temporized. "Have I told you that Wagner is my favorite, or did you just guess?"

"Good, then. I have the tickets right here."

Doberman gulped. He was not used to crossing partners. "It's a wonderful opera. I especially love the aria that opens the third act." (He hoped there was one.) "But this is, this is not the best time. I have a very important matter to work on. They've given me the key section of a brief that's due Monday."

Cinders was more baffled than anything else. No associate at the firm had contradicted him in any way for more than twenty years. He decided that perhaps Doberman did not understand.

"I'm asking a favor, in addition to giving one," he explained. "I have a lunch meeting next week with the Friends of the Opera. My tablemates, including at least one potential client, know I have tickets and will want to discuss it. They will expect me to know the plot and names of the singers, and perhaps to comment on the production."

By now, Doberman was writhing in torment. Not ordinarily a religious man, he began to wonder if Heaven was punishing him for his fake conversation with Cinders less than an hour earlier.

Cinders shifted to a more sympathetic tone. "Be that as it may. I understand that you have other responsibilities. Perhaps some other young fellow can help me. Are there any other opera buffs among the associates? What about Stellworth?"

Doberman turned a pale shade of green, with orange and gray spots around the temples. In a hollow, strangled tone, far from his usual vivacity, he accepted the invitation, and assured Cinders that it really was no problem at all.

Only after hanging up did he realize the ridiculously obvious solution to his problem. Someone would have to go to the opera, but it did not have to be him. There was always Lyla. Of course, this would require a skilled presentation and careful handling. Thinking of the difficulties that might be involved after their last conversation, Doberman decided to indulge in the pleasure of boasting to Stellworth first.

Stellworth was just hanging up the phone on his wife and turning to a stack of papers on his desk when Doberman entered his office. He winced and blinked his eyes angrily, but Doberman just smiled.

"Are you staying late tonight?" asked the soul of geniality.
"What do you think?"
"Me, too. I won't be able to work the entire weekend."
Stellworth did not bother to answer. Avid a gossip though

he might be about Doberman's personal life behind Doberman's back, he was not the sort of person who would stoop to asking a direct question.

After the proper dramatic pause, Doberman explained that Cinders had simply insisted that he go to see *Der Meistersinger* on Sunday.

Stellworth could not help himself. "You're going with Cinders to the opera?"

Doberman corrected him gently. "Not with him. Instead of him. He couldn't go, but said he knew I would enjoy it. It's very flattering - I gather he's anxious to hear my opinion about the performance."

Despite the crushing weight of this disclosure, Stellworth rallied. It occurred to him that Doberman's phone colloquy during the associates' meeting about the Barlow case had included no mention of the opera. And even Doberman couldn't wheedle two invitations from Mr. Cinders for the same weekend.

"I thought you were going to an art exhibit."

"Art exhibit?" Doberman said slowly. "I don't remember discussing an art exhibit..." He paused and then nodded as if the reference had suddenly become clear to him. "Lowell, I'm sure you didn't mean to, but I think you've been eavesdropping."

To Doberman's surprise, Stellworth let this pass. This was a bad sign - Stellworth must be thinking of something, since usually he rose to the bait.

In fact, Stellworth was thinking of something, and he was thinking hard. Something was fishy, and he thought he knew what.

As luck would have it, however, Stellworth had overlooked the most promising angle. Believing implicitly in the reality of the phone conversation that he thought he had overheard, he let his suspicions focus on the opera. He could not believe that Doberman would be going, and seriously doubted the invitation. While rejecting direct interrogation of Cinders as

25

too risky for now, he resolved to follow the situation closely. Just let Doberman try to boast about attending *Der Meistersinger* if Stellworth caught him in the library on Sunday night.

Doberman, meanwhile, was pondering the terms of his approach to Lyla as he trotted down the hallway. There were two possibilities. One was to say that he unexpectedly found he might have time, and would love to take her to the opera on Sunday night if his work progressed satisfactorily. He would provide bulletins and updates, then finally beg off and suggest that she take her mother.

The second, more forthright, approach would be to say right away that he could not make it but thought she might be interested. Much as he detested forthrightness, Doberman decided that this time it was unavoidable.

To Doberman's relief, Lyla answered the phone when he called, thus sparing him the ordeal of talking to Doris. Lyla was touched by his thoughtfulness in asking Mr. Cinders for tickets so that she and her mother could go to the opera, although she feared it would be boring.

"Can mother take one of her friends instead of me?" she asked.

"But Lyla, the idea was to give you something to do together. Since you'll both be missing me. Anyway, I need you to report to me about it. Cinders thinks I'm going and he's likely to ask me questions."

Lyla's tone dropped about 50 degrees Fahrenheit, or 27.8 degrees Celsius.

"Let me get this straight. You're not offering me a favor, you're asking for one. And right after you canceled on me for tonight with twenty seconds' notice."

Doberman paused for a moment, and decided it was time to play the sexual jealousy card. This was an emotion that he regarded with something of the puzzlement that a Neanderthal might feel in a conversation about second mortgages and timeshares. Still, he had learned that it could be effective on her, used judiciously.

"That's only part of it," he said. "I was also looking for a quiet place to work, and I thought your apartment would be ideal if both of you went out for the evening. Maybe I could see you afterwards. I don't want to work at home or in the law firm because too many people would be bothering me. Still, if you don't want to go to the opera, I guess I should find someplace else."

"Like where?"

Doberman was as vague as possible. The only thing more dangerous than arousing too much jealousy is completely dispelling it. He was not surprised when Lyla capitulated, promising to go to the opera with her mother and report to him afterwards, so long as he would work in her apartment and stay out of trouble.

4. Interlude

Ashby & Cinders, late that Friday night, bore little resemblance to a house on the night before Christmas. Creatures were stirring on each of its three floors, and the library periodically swelled with whispering until someone would hiss for silence.

While Doberman gladhanded his way through the library like a campaigning politician, and Stellworth ostentatiously sidled through every few minutes holding a cup of coffee, Porter was sitting isolated in his office. He had never grasped that half the reason for working late hours was simply to be seen there.

Every few minutes, Porter would stare into space, wearying of the bulky documents he had to digest by Sunday morning in order to have time to write. He looked like the canary that had just been eaten by the cat.

Why am I here, he asked himself for the millionth time. The question could be answered at many levels. Because I took the Metro here this morning. Because they seemed nice when I was a summer associate. Bad luck. Failure of imagination. Masochism. Or maybe just because I have a family to feed and

28

Janet's part-time social work salary hardly pays for daycare plus an occasional nice dinner.

He had not planned to be a lawyer from the get-go. Butterflies must first be caterpillars, but Porter was living proof that lawyers need not start out as pre-laws. A Columbia 1969 college graduate – people still sometimes raised their eyebrows at this, recalling the days of rage – he could well remember when "pre-law" had been a dirty word. At least, it was unless you said you were planning to use it against "the Man." Most of the people who had said that in 1969 were law firm partners now.

Back in college, Porter had been used to hearing the slogan, in relation to the student protests, that if you're not with us you're against us. They might have had him in mind, an excited but cautious watcher on the sidelines and on television. Still, slogans are just that even when people are still mouthing them. Porter had felt he had a kind of honorary non-combatant status, as a dreamer who could quietly plan for graduate school in American history without facing any worse condemnation than: Don't you realize how things are changing? Or, you're not really with it. But some people said: Cool, you can shake up the universities from the other side and write about how fascist our country has always been. Are you going to study slavery? The Industrial Revolution? One or the other, he'd say.

Only after three years of graduate school and another year sitting at home had Porter decided that detailed historical research and writing weren't really his thing, likewise lecturing to undergraduates, although he rather liked poking through old archives. This seemed to leave law school as the natural or at least default choice. No blood and bodily wastes like in medical school; no flow charts, corporate marketing plans, and need to develop your golf game if you wanted to get anywhere, like in business school.

He had gone to law school at Yale, where, in a fit of post-1960s faculty cowering, or maybe it was smart product placement versus Harvard (New Haven was no Cambridge), they had eliminated nearly all grade differentiation. Having just Honors and Pass for people to think about had been a relief to Porter, not because he could not get good grades - he generally could - but because atmospherically it was a kind of shark repellent. No surprise that Doberman had gone to Harvard. Then again, Porter thought, maybe it would have helped me at A & C if I had met the sharks a bit earlier, or more precisely if the sharks who went there anyway had swum a bit closer and given me earlier survival training.

The best thing in law school had been meeting Janet, then an exchange student spending a semester at the Yale Divinity School. But take two lonely and well-matched individuals, add eight years, with the luck of the draw producing two very active little boys, and what it apparently yielded was a weekend at the A & C library, buried beyond escape in meeting large responsibilities. Right now Janet was probably trying to get the boys to bed. They might be asking "Where's Daddy?" unless they had already forgotten about him.

The hours passed. The clock struck midnight and Porter labored on, making notes on index cards that he hoped he would be able to read later. This was dull stuff, all about standard deviations and double blind studies. Oh, for a bit of conflict of laws or Administrative Procedure Act litigation - something he could really dig into.

Stellworth at midnight was grimly scouring his files, debating whether memos written long ago by departed associates could be trusted as shortcuts for his research. Normally he would have scorned such expedients, but if he did not get a couple of hours of sleep it would probably show in his work later. Disgusting it was, really, to be so weak.

Hopefully Sarah would be asleep when he got home, maybe not much past four in the morning. If she woke up even at that hour, she was bound to start telling him about her day. Either that, or she would want to discuss his parents' impending visit and how to handle the inevitable question about whether they were planning to have children soon. The answer was definitely no, they agreed on that, but he didn't want to spend needed sleep time discussing the fine points of how best to squelch the would-be grandparents yet satisfy their natural curiosity within fair limits.

Sarah could go on for hours, he would think in disloyal moments when he felt stretched on the rack a bit by work pressures. At other times he would think, thank goodness she keeps the conversation going. I can just listen and agree with her as needed. That's easy enough for me since usually she sees things the right way. He had recognized this attribute of hers the first time they ever spoke, at an eleventh grade dinner dance hosted by his prep school for its sister school, where she went.

"Isn't this a stupid dance?" she had said to him by the punch bowl. "I didn't even want to come." It was hard to say whether he had been more struck by how right she was, how fully he agreed, or how well she must understand him even though until that moment they had never exchanged a word.

Stellworth began to doze. He would wake up in a few minutes and head back to the coffee room. Plainly his trips there would need to be more frequent from this point on.

Doberman at midnight was doing the best of the three associates, exulting in a promising line of cases that he had just discovered. They seemed to suggest at least circumstantially that all risks in a given class are covered when any of them is warned against. The question was how you defined such a class. If he could find anything helpful on this point, the cases could play a role in his argument even though none of them involved federal administrative or regulatory issues. Doberman headed for Crossley's office, half to see if Crossley was there and half to boast if he was. Good luck; he was standing in front of the desk with his back to the door, head down and rooting through a stack of papers.

"Peter! I'm surprised to see you here this late!"

Crossley started, spun around, saw Doberman, and grunted. He had just stopped in on his way home from a tedious dinner party. The talk there had been endless about such topics as whether Senator Baker and the White House were falling out, and whether Senator Kennedy would ever run for President again. The problem wasn't the topics or the time spent on them – he liked political chat as much as the next Capital Hill dinner party guest, which was saying a lot – but rather the evident skepticism in the room that a K Street lawyer might have anything illuminating to say about them. Back at the office, all he meant to do was grab his copies of the week's Wall Street Journals and perhaps quickly spy on the associates before his wife Anne got too restive waiting in the car.

"Still, I can hardly blame you, with such a lovely office," Doberman continued. "If I had an office like this, I'd probably live in it."

"I can't talk now," said Crossley quickly, tensing lest Doberman try to nudge him in the ribs. As Crossley fled, Doberman went to the window to examine the famous view that "looked like Paris." Then he sat in Crossley's chair, put his feet on the desk, and posed with his arms folded behind his neck. I'd like it here, he thought. A moment later, he was dozing.

5. The Lost Weekend

Saturday began to the gloomy accompaniment of blue skies and sparkling sunshine. At least, everyone on the team assigned to the Barlow case found this gloomy, although each for different reasons.

For Crossley, the weather meant a trip to the country with Anne to visit her parents. He had been hoping for April showers, or maybe a cold front, to provide him with an excuse for postponing the trip, but here it was above 70 degrees on April 2, and therefore here he was.

Doberman and Porter hated the weather because they had to spend the entire day in the office, rather than also having time to play tennis in Rock Creek Park or do yard work, respectively. Stellworth simply hated nice weather. It was an article of faith with him from his Boston upbringing that only cold, drizzly weather, preferably with an overlay of fog, was respectable.

Adding to the day's indignity for Crossley, Anne had warned him, in a tone that he knew meant business, to be on his best behavior. Jim Hankins, an important aide to Senator Bentsen - the second ranking Democrat on the Finance Committee!

- would be stopping by for the day with his wife Jill, Anne's former college roommate. Rumor had it that Hankins might be moving to the Democratic National Committee for next year's Presidential election. Crossley ought to try to fascinate him - as Anne knew he easily could if he put his mind to it - if not for his own sake, and the connection might always be useful, then at least for hers.

Doggedly he did her bidding, batting his eyes and doling out excruciating smiles while he portrayed himself as an important legal player on behalf of the tobacco industry. Barlow Industries, it turned out, had oil interests in Texas and was close to Senator Bentsen, or at least they should know that his door was always open to them. Every now and then Crossley would be left alone for long enough to unwind by throwing a furtive rock at a bird or squirrel.

The three associates, meanwhile, were spending all day in the library. Still, even if they were not directly communing with nature like Crossley, at least they could do the next best thing by watching each other like beasts of the jungle. Stellworth in particular was carefully tracking the progress of Doberman's research, in preparation for verifying his timely departure on Sunday for the opera.

There reputedly are hunters, be they Indians or the gruff English types featured in Hemingway-style homoerotic fantasies, who possess incredible skill in tracing even the faintest or oldest wild animal spoor. They can track bears across streams, or sense a lion's recent presence even if its pawprints have been eradicated by a herd of wildebeests.

Stellworth's skills were not of this order, but then again they did not have to be. When he saw a pile of lawbooks, piled precariously and studded with paperclips, it was almost childishly obvious that Doberman had started intensive research. Stellworth could watch as the pile periodically shrank due to the ministrations of the Xerox room, and expanded as Doberman did more research.

The other important clues that Stellworth could rely upon included the amount of underlining on Xeroxed pages, the index cards which Doberman used to organize cases, the yellow legal pads that he covered with a scrawl incomprehensible to all but a few secretaries, and a research guide known as Shepard's. Since this landmark of the accumulated wisdom of our civilization is not widely known outside of the legal profession, perhaps it should briefly be described.

Shepard's is an extended index showing, for every case or other source of legal authority, every instance in which it has ever been cited in another such authority. For example, suppose that Crossley, just once, had surrendered to his deepest instincts and tortured his neighbor's cat, leading to a police summons and subsequent proceedings shedding light on the Miranda warning. The resulting court opinion would have appeared in Shepard's (identified only by the volume and page number at which it was printed). The listing would identify the volume and page numbers at which all appeals, reversals, and remands were listed, as well as every page at which it had been cited in another case. Shepard's can be used, not only to determine whether a case is still good law, but also to accumulate huge lists of cases relating to the same subject. One case may cite twenty more, which Shepard's reveals have each been cited by twenty more, and so on as the client's bill approaches infinity. While soon to become a one-click computer search, Shepard's at this time remained the name of an actual set of bulky volumes on the library shelves, which associates had to consult laboriously whenever they needed to check citations.

The associates at Ashby & Cinders derived much innocent merriment from the thought of the poor anonymous drones who must do the updating of Shepard's for newly decided cases - much as the souls in a medieval version of Hell might have enjoyed watching the torments of those in lower circles, if this pleasure had not been so thoughtfully restricted to the souls in Heaven. Still, the torment of Shepard's was not restricted to these anonymous drones. Shepard's was so familiar a part of the average associate's life that it had entered the language as a verb: one "shepardized" a case, or all the citations in a document.

As Saturday progressed, Stellworth, that tireless shepardizer, continually had to stop himself from sneering at Doberman's more ramshackle approach to legal research. Stellworth had recently noticed in a mirror that his first wrinkles were beginning to appear along the often-used sneer lines around his mouth, and he accordingly was rationing himself strictly.

Still, even as he cautiously essayed a few mirthless snickers that he hoped would be non-hazardous, Stellworth could not suppress a twinge of icy fear about Doberman's progress. Doberman, when working, always looked and sounded something like Sherlock Holmes at the scene of a murder. He would pace around intently, peering closely at Xeroxed cases and muttering ejaculations like "Of course!" or "How stupid!" Then he would swoop into the stacks for another casebook, and dash back to his chair to scribble furiously for a few more minutes.

Confronted by this performance, Stellworth's officecraft failed him. For all the muttering and scribbling, the weekend was not going well for Doberman when he left the office on Sunday to establish his operatic alibi. Behind the nonchalant exterior he always sought to present in moments of crisis, he was feeling positively chalant.

Associates writing legal briefs under time pressure, no less than tennis players at Wimbledon, go through up and down stretches. On some days they cannot move well and miss easy putaways. Everything seems difficult and clumsy, and takes twice as long.

So it was with Doberman as he struggled to write about assumption of risk. He had difficulty focusing his research amid the vast sea of available cases. Once he began writing, he had trouble achieving the proper tone. The draft kept coming out either too callous towards cancer victims or too sympathetic, whereas he needed to convey that the tobacco company cared very deeply about health problems but that the Commissioners should not. Moreover, with all the shortcuts forced upon him by time constraints, he was haunted by the fear that he would be the one to break the Ashby & Cinders record of error-free brief-writing.

Even worse than the suffering itself was the way he had to wallow in it for the benefit of Lyla, who, still hoping to entice him to the opera, kept calling for progress reports. While she hated complaining other than her own and was not deeply interested in the progress of the Barlow brief, she felt constrained to listen as a means of establishing his bona fides. After years of hearing him boast about what a great lawyer he was, Lyla found it hard to believe that he was having so much difficulty, and increasingly suspected him of secret plans for Sunday night that he hoped to conceal by sending her to the opera.

Despite both Lyla and the work-related obstacles, Doberman had made enough progress by Sunday night that he could begin to see the possibility of finishing. Still, it would be a tedious and horrible struggle at best.

"I wish I didn't have so much revising to do," he told Lyla on a private phone line, secure from Stellworth, shortly before his departure. "As it is, I still have two sections to write – probably at least ten pages."

Doberman's unease, however, arose from more than the sheer volume of work. In order to have a draft on Crossley's desk by 9 on Monday morning without staying in the office on Sunday night, he would have to surmount several difficulties. For one, there was Lyla's inexcusable lack of a law library in her apartment to assist him in his research. Doberman had prepared for this difficulty by squirreling away Xeroxed cases in his briefcase. More serious was the apartment's lack of adequate support capacity, in the form of secretaries and word processors.

Without such capacity, he could not hope to have everything typed by zero hour even if he finished writing in time. Thus, he was forced to contemplate a risky fraud. At 9 o'clock on Monday, he would give Crossley a draft that included only the sections he had already written by the time he left the office on Sunday. In presenting this purportedly final version, he would loudly praise himself for finishing on time. An updated and completed draft would then be smuggled in and substituted for it as soon as possible.

As he described the intended substitution to Lyla, Doberman could almost hear Crossley's voice, softly asking him why he could not have been more honest and trusting. He could also hear a much louder voice: Lyla's, interrupting the description of the intended scam in order to discuss the upcoming evening.

"You'll definitely stay in my house the whole time?" she asked him.

"Of course. What else would I be doing?"

"I wouldn't know. But I'll call you during the intermission, just to see how you're doing."

"Great."

"One more thing. My mother isn't going with me after all - "

Doberman blanched, turned pale, felt his heart skip a beat, gulped, gasped, and swallowed. He could picture the old bat looming over him in sinister triumph as he struggled with writer's block.

"- but don't worry. When she heard that you'd be visiting, she decided to spend the evening in a friend's house. You should really try to cultivate her more."

There was a pause, while Doberman in silent prayer thanked the gods and pledged his first-born in gratitude.

"Don't you want to know who I'm going with?"

"I can't imagine."

"Gidget O'Malley."

Doberman, realizing that he was entering deep waters, hastened to express a warm yet wholly disinterested gratification. The Gidget O'Malley issue was one that had lingered at the edges of his dealings with Lyla for some weeks now, and was best left there.

Gidget O'Malley was a recently arrived Ashby & Cinders secretary, working on a floor where Doberman's work seldom took him, but to whom Lyla believed he had taken a fancy. The accusation was ridiculous, particularly since such a fancy would be so contrary to Doberman's self-interest. To act on such a fancy, if it existed, would endanger, not only Doberman's relationship with Lyla, but his standing in the law firm. Dating a secretary was discouraged in any case, and doing so after a relationship with a paralegal, which itself was only quasi-legal, would be even worse. What made the accusation even more ridiculous was the fact that Gidget O'Malley was not (as Doberman emphasized to Lyla) "my type."

Certainly she was not Lyla's physical type. In the tale of the tape, Lyla had a couple of extra inches to Gidget's maybe six or eight extra pounds. If the one was all straight lines, the other was all rounded and soft. Their carriages were also very different. Gidget slouched a bit, and looking at her one might rightly have suspected that at some point she had followed the Grateful Dead. She had easy manners - too easy for where she now found herself - and a disturbing tendency towards sincerity and naturalness, for which, in the corporate law firm setting, she tended to be disdained.

Gidget had long reddish auburn hair that she wore curled with bangs in the front, the whole framed by golden hoop earrings. Her bright eyes, with which she made frequent (but smiling, not aggressive) eye contact, were close-set in her broad round face, and close as well to a petite snub nose and full lips. Since she wore a bit of lipstick and slightly rouged her cheeks,

Doberman could say to Lyla that she wore too much makeup, but he knew this was unfair, and merely a convenient talking point since Lyla wore none. He had felt he needed talking points since the time Lyla caught him staring at Gidget's breasts. They were almost worth it, jutting out roundly close together and still high-set. Thinking fast, he had told Lyla that he was merely wondering whether they would pose a problem for Gidget if she did aerobics.

The low-cut tops that Gidget favored were within the acceptable limits of law firm decorum but perhaps just barely. She would match them with skirts to the knee or above, brightly colored and with bold flowered patterns unless she needed a solid to go with a flowered top. Yet if her sartorial taste was very definite, her presentation was often casual. Blouses might have a wrinkle or two, or be permitted as she wore them to come untucked in the back.

The opera invitation must have come as a surprise to her. Perhaps she had accepted due to the novelty or because she did not have many friends in Washington yet, having only recently moved from somewhere near San Diego. But to Doberman, with his greater knowledge of the surrounding circumstances, it was as clear as a bell - and an unusually clear one at that - exactly what Lyla was thinking in making the invitation. Her plan, much like Crossley's during his weekend in the country but less literally, was to kill two birds with one stone. By inviting Gidget, Lyla hoped, not only to avoid inflicting boredom on her mother, but to keep Doberman away from Gidget on Sunday night. She also might be hoping to probe a bit, and perhaps to plant a seed of reluctance to respond favorably to any overtures that he might subsequently make. The cleverest thing about it was that Doberman could not even reproach Lyla for her lack of trust without implicitly conceding that the issue of his possibly initiating relations with Gidget actually existed.

Under the circumstances, there was nothing for Doberman

to do but repair quietly to Lyla's apartment and begin his evening's labor. So off he went, and for some time he was pleasantly surprised by the improvement over working in the Ashby & Cinders library. Without Stellworth to stare down or the other lawyers to gladhand or impress, Doberman found that he could actually concentrate better on what he was doing. He had completed sweeping revisions of the sections from the office and written two pages of the remaining portion when disaster struck.

It happened in the middle of a footnote. Doberman was executing that Ashby & Cinders specialty, the "string cite" (a citation of twenty or so cases to illustrate a single narrow point), when he noticed that a stack of five district court cases, fastened with a paper clip so that he would remember to use them together, had not been shepardized.

Some people, at this juncture, would have panicked. One can imagine Napoleon throwing a temper tantrum and blaming his marshals. Perhaps James Bond would have shed the tiniest drop of perspiration. Doberman, however, responded to crisis in the only way he knew: by reaching for a yellow legal pad.

Bringing his racing thoughts under control, Doberman proceeded, with a barely shaking hand, to write and underline the word "Options" at the top, and then to list the alternatives.

"1. Omit the 5 cases."

Impossible. Despite all the other cases in the string cite, Doberman needed these five. The others were included chiefly to impress the client with his thoroughness. These five cases were the ones Doberman actually intended to discuss in text.

"2. Include them as is."

Equally impossible. If just one of the cases was no more than innocuously confirmed by the appeals court - an optimistic scenario - Doberman would still be the person who broke the A & C record of error-free brief-writing.

"3. Include them now, and shepardize them tomorrow."

This was more promising, but still not good enough. It made little sense to write about a decision and then potentially discover that it had been overturned. Anyway, Doberman's Monday would be perilous enough already, what with planning to have an updated draft surreptitiously typed and smuggled into Crossley's office. He was reluctant to increase the danger through direct communications with the secretary who was doing the secret typing.

"4. Go for it."

In other words, make an immediate break for the A & C library, and shepardize the cases before writing another word. Needless to say, he would have to do this without being seen, since ostensibly he was at the opera.

This was the Rambo approach - a secret raid behind enemy lines, with no hope of mercy if he was captured. Indeed, it was riskier than the Rambo approach, since Rambo did not have to worry that a jealous girlfriend would call while he was out slaughtering Communists. Still, there seemed to be no alternative.

Lacking a false moustache or the power to cloud men's minds, Doberman knew that he would have to be extremely careful in carrying out this operation. Ashby & Cinders usually thinned out at least slightly on Sundays after dinner, but it would not be empty. In particular, Stellworth would surely be there - Stellworth, who, if he discovered what Doberman was up to, would react like a starving, rabid timber wolf that has finally cornered a peasant whose taunting and wisecracks it has long bitterly resented.

Leaving quickly, Doberman arrived within fifteen minutes at a corner of K Street across from where the law firm was located. Tipping the cabbie generously for luck, he headed stealthily toward the building, surveying the passers-by as he walked. To his relief, the security card that he needed for night entrance to the building worked immediately. He advanced into the lobby, pressed the button for an elevator, and hid behind a column. There was a long pause. Finally an elevator arrived and opened its sliding doors. Just as Doberman started to step out, he saw two Ashby & Cinders associates emerge. By the time they had left the lobby, the elevator was gone.

Doberman pressed for the elevator again, and again retreated behind his column. This time the wait was even longer. By the time the elevator arrived, Doberman was in no mood to take it. An elevator, he realized, was a cul de sac, with no place to hide or exit if he should arrive at a floor infested with more associates. So, clutching his building key, he headed for the stairs.

The library was twelve flights up, and Doberman's physical condition was not what it had been during his college days. Anxious to avoid fatigue and heavy breathing, he took his time, pausing whenever he felt winded. Eventually he arrived at the proper floor. Here, cautiously inserting his building key into the lock, he opened the door enough to peer into the darkened hallway.

All was clear. Still, Doberman paused for a moment to review the physical steps that lay ahead. First, he would have to dart across the hallway and find the security lock. By inserting the A & C security key, he would turn off the little red light and give himself sixty seconds to open the library door without setting off an alarm. Next, he would have to cross the hall again and use his A & C door key to enter the library. Finally, if possible, he would have to turn the alarm back on and head deep into the shelves where he could hide if he heard footsteps.

Everything worked as planned. Doberman entered the library and snuck behind some little-used shelves containing cases from defunct administrative agencies. Here he paused, within earshot of several voices, to consider his next move.

The library was a large, musty, and for the most part dimly lit room consisting of narrow, intersecting rows of stacked books, along with two open areas, one large and one small, at which there were desks and better lighting. For Doberman, of course, this lighting was a hostile force, and he cursed it.

There were three sets of Shepard's in the library that listed Federal district court cases. The first, kept by the main set of desks, plainly was inaccessible under the circumstances. The second, by the smaller open area, was dangerous as well. While there were only four desks there, which might well be unoccupied, the lighting would create substantial risk. Moreover, if he moved the volumes to a darker area, it was possible that someone else would go looking for them.

The third set of Shepard's was kept at the back, in a dark area not far from where Doberman was standing. The problem with this set was that it was regarded as a spare. Accordingly, it was likely enough to be missing a volume or the latest update.

Doberman was on the verge of sidling towards this set of volumes when he heard a horrible sound. It was Stellworth's voice, coming from only a few rows away.

"Nadine, could you come here for a moment?" The polite, mincing tone sounded like an invitation to waltz, yet one could hear the steel underneath.

There was a scurrying noise as the librarian hastened to comply.

"You know how sorry I am to make you come in this late," Stellworth continued. "I know it's beyond the regular call of duty. But once you're here, I would hope that you'd be as thorough as I'm sure you are at any other time."

"Is anything wrong?" she countered feebly.

"Is anything wrong?" His tone, if anything, doubled in sweetness. "I asked you for twelve specific books, and you said that one of them was missing. Now I find it here in the back, among the extra sets."

After a few more edifying observations, Stellworth released her and ambled back to the front of the library. Nadine lingered for a few more seconds, groaning softly to herself, and then followed him out of the area.

The knowledge that his enemy was in the field dampened Doberman's confidence for a moment, until it occurred to him how much sweeter the triumph would be if wrested from Stellworth so boldly (albeit that no one would ever know). So, taking a deep breath and thrusting his chin forward, Doberman advanced to the very shelves where Stellworth had only recently been standing.

Fortunately for Doberman, the crucial volumes of Shepard's were located on a shelf by the floor near a corner, thus permitting him to slip into an adjoining aisle if disturbed. He crouched on the floor near the books and removed from his pocket a paper on which he had written the citations for the five cases.

The first case had been decided in 1952. This ancient date (in law, almost anything decided more than twenty years ago is ancient), along with the cumbersome manner in which Shepard's was organized, exposed Doberman to inconvenience. Given the cost of hard printing and binding, there could be no one Shepard's covering the entire period since 1952, and, even if there briefly had been, it would rapidly have become obsolete as new cases were decided. Thus, in order thoroughly to shepardize this case, Doberman was obliged to consult in sequence a succession of volumes.

First, there was an immense navy blue tome covering the years from 1943 to 1971. From this volume, Doberman learned that the case had been affirmed by the appeals court and that a writ of certiorari to the United States Supreme Court had been sought but denied. After writing this down, he turned to a tome of similar weight and color, covering the years from 1971 to 1976. Here he learned that the case had been only sporadically cited, but never overturned, and questioned in only one instance, by a circuit he could afford to ignore. Next, he examined a softbound yellow volume,

covering the period until almost the present time. Here there
was nothing of importance. But even now the case was not
fully shepardized. There was still a slim red-covered pamphlet,
covering cases decided in the last few months. This pamphlet
was not to be found.

It was unlikely that the red pamphlet, covering such a
short period, contained anything of importance. Still, as a
true son of Ashby & Cinders, Doberman felt that it had to be
checked. He decided to shepardize the other four cases, using
the available volumes, and then to seek the red pamphlet by
the smaller set of desks.

Proceeding to the second case, Doberman began to sink
into the dull trance state in which shepardization is best
accomplished. Thus, he was startled when suddenly footsteps
sounded only yards away. With several bulky volumes on his
lap, he was ill-equipped to move rapidly. Still, he dove for the
corner, letting the volumes slip to the floor, and disappeared
only an instant before Stellworth entered the row of shelves
again.

Doberman cowered in silence as he listened to Stellworth
rummaging around among the books. Stellworth had returned,
apparently, to restore the missing book that he had shown to
Nadine. Once there, however, seeing the volumes of Shepard's
lying scattered on the floor, he grunted angrily and stooped to
restore them to their proper places. Doberman realized that he
was lost if Stellworth should decide to look for the miscreant.
An excruciating moment passed before Stellworth turned and
sauntered back to the front of the library.

Quickly returning to his place, Doberman resumed
shepardizing the list of cases. After his narrow escape, however,
he no longer had the heart to search for the red pamphlet.
Yet the last of the five cases, *Tomcat Industries v. Maryland
Consumer Counsel*, raised the possibility that he would have
to after all. Decided recently and Doberman's favorite of
the bunch – it found assumption of risk of increased blood

pressure (and therefore heart attack risk) by users of an over-the-counter diet pill that merely contained a general health warning ("Check with your physician ...") - it gave rise to only two citations, both in the softbound yellow volume. The first gave a page and volume number, along with the letter "a." This meant that the case had been affirmed by the appeals court. The second line noted that a motion for appellate rehearing had been filed by one of the parties, and not yet acted on by the volume's date of publication.

Would Doberman have to brave the open areas of the library after all, seeking the red pamphlet, despite the perils he had already encountered on much more favorable terrain? Upon reflection, he decided not. Petitions for rehearing are filed routinely by parties that have lost in appellate litigation, and just as routinely are denied. Persuading a court to change its mind after it has issued a published opinion is on a par with persuading an umpire that a pitch that he already called strike three was actually an inch off the plate. The only reason lawyers even file motions for rehearing, in many cases, is to boost their fees a bit and show that no possible step has been omitted.

With this in mind, Doberman restored the books to their shelves, crept to the door, and within minutes had vanished into the night. He found a cab immediately, returned to Lyla's building, and was just coming up to the door when he heard her phone ringing, ringing, ringing, and falling silent before he could get there.

6. The Morning After

Back in Lyla's apartment, Doberman waited for a few minutes in the hope that she would call right back. He planned to let the phone ring about three times and then to answer it breathlessly, as if interrupted in mid-sentence, with the hope of convincing her that he had been working the whole time and that on her previous attempt she must have dialed a wrong number.

When the phone did not ring again, Doberman gathered his papers and left for his own apartment. He had too much work ahead of him to contemplate engaging in a scene as well. Before leaving, he wrote a brief note explaining to Lyla that he had sadly been unable to answer what he assumed was her call (detained, a tastefully veiled hint suggested, by digestive problems), but would be at home if she wished to try again.

Throughout the night, as his phone remained ominously silent, Doberman toiled on. He finished in time to down a strong pot of instant coffee and arrive at the office by 6 in the morning. Here he distributed his two drafts for typing, both the official one to be finished by 9 and the real one to be finished when possible. He then collapsed in a conference room for a brief nap.

At precisely 8:59 a.m., Doberman arrived at Crossley's office with the bogus draft in hand. Stellworth, emerging at that very moment, paused to give him a look of withering scorn, the fruits of victory earned by having arrived at 8:57.

Doberman chose to ignore this gesture. Striding boldly through the door, he put a hand to his lips to still the seated Crossley, and assumed a dramatic pose by the double window. From here, he inhaled deeply, as if he could smell fresh air even though the window was permanently sealed.

Turning to Crossley with a grin he winked, and said, pointing to the view: "This is why we do it, Peter, isn't it."

"Excuse me?"

"This is why we sweat blood and spend long weekends getting everything just right - not that I don't love the pure challenge. But it's an office like this, along with everything else that you've achieved, that really - "

"Sweating blood?" Crossley interjected. "Lowell tells me that you've been spending your time at the opera."

Doberman felt that this comment called for a disarming smile. Like a true Method actor, he summoned the necessary emotion by contemplating how Stellworth would look disembowelled.

"Oh, yes. I got the basics done early so I'd have time to let it percolate a bit. I thought a light break, like some Wagner, would do some good."

While relieved to be so glib under pressure, Doberman was under no illusion that he had dispelled the Stellworth poison. Among other things, the news about the opera might suggest that Doberman had been less than thorough in writing his section of the brief. And Crossley would close in quickly if he smelled blood.

Doberman accordingly broadened his grin until his lips began to hurt. "The reason I mention your success, Peter, is that I really feel I'm learning from you. I wrote this brief just the way I thought that you would want it. And I hope you'll notice."

"You can be sure that I will read it carefully."

"Will you? That would be great! In fact, I really hope you'll read it through twice before you start the hard editing. Once before you read Porter's piece on the scientific evidence - that's not here yet? Funny, it's 9:04--"

"Only 9:01."

"--and once afterwards. I'd really like you to see how I've interwoven it with the evidence."

Crossley, wincing, promised to give it his careful attention, and placed it on a stack of papers. He began fingering the Stellworth section, which he evidently now planned to read first. Thus encouraged, Doberman withdrew, just in time to leave the field to a puffing, red-faced Porter.

With the Western front now stable for the moment, Doberman turned back to the Eastern front. He headed for Lyla's cubicle, weighing as he walked the likely cost of the dinner and show that might be needed to placate her.

Ordinarily, in the absence of a compelling purpose like his need for information about the opera, Doberman would not have bothered her so soon after a disturbance. He once had analyzed her moods as involving four levels of ascending irritability. Level 1 defined the state when she was in a good mood and her company was enjoyable. At Level 2, she was just irritable enough to be no fun, but not so upset as to require soothing. Once she reached Level 3, he considered it important to placate her. Finally, at Level 4 she was so irate that it was best to steer clear until she subsided to a lower level. Fortunately, a kind of pyramid effect made each ascending level less common than the one below it.

With his quick, practiced glance, Doberman was able to make a barometric reading before exchanging a single word. She was definitely at Level 5.

Lyla did not answer his cheery hello, preferring to demonstrate that she was too absorbed in the scientific evidence file that she was collating for Porter to pay him any attention. Having started the confrontation, however, he decided to press forward.

"Well, Lyla, I'm feeling much better today."

She still did not see or hear him.

"Of course, I'm going to be careful. After that terrible upset stomach I had last night in your place, it's nothing but rice and cottage cheese for me today."

The silence continued.

"But tomorrow night, I was wondering if you'd like to try that new Austrian restaurant on 13th Street. I hear it's pretty expensive, but what the hell."

At this, Lyla looked up, if only for a moment. Doberman decided to press his advantage.

"You could have schnitzel," he wheedled. "It's a kind of pot roast. Bottle of wine - maybe some Liebfraumilch - black forest cheese cake -"

"Can't you see that I'm busy?" She resumed collating documents.

Too late, Doberman remembered that she hated cheese cake. He thought of trying apple streudel, but the moment for bribery had passed.

Doberman had too much pride to grovel, unless he thought it might do him some good. Accordingly, after a few more moments of being ignored, he returned to his office.

He arrived there just in time to get a phone call from Cinders' secretary. The great man wanted to see him immediately, presumably to talk about the opera.

Without the benefit of Lyla's eyewitness account, Doberman realized that he would have to keep it general. Fortunately, he had cribbed some catchphrases from an opera book for this very contingency. What he had not prepared for, however, was the sight of Stellworth, seated in Cinders' office, with no apparent intention of leaving and the air of an avenging angel.

Cinders was bolt upright at his desk, showing Doberman a jaunty smile and a jauntier pink bowtie.

"So, my young friend," he burbled. "Did you have a pleasant evening?"

"It was exquisite! And I feel so grateful about it - not just for the opportunity, but for, how shall I put it, the compliment?"

Stellworth flinched. Somehow it seems we always end up hurting the ones we hate.

Cinders frowned, intent on getting down to business. "You liked the production?"

"How can I begin? It was so ... so thoroughly symphonic. It had a certain, I don't know what it was, but it was a certain je ne sais quoi."

Cinders nodded, muttering "Good, good," but obviously expecting more.

"So ripe in texture. The almost cinematic drive. The - the use of unresolved chromaticism."

"Good, good."

"It makes - I hope I am not going overboard - even Verdi seem, how shall I put it, dare I say insensitive, almost gauche?"

"Good. But tell me about the production."

Doberman shrugged expressively, making what was probably a moue, if the definition in a recent crossword puzzle ("Pierre's pout") was correct. Meanwhile, Stellworth, in the corner, had turned a dull purple, with orange trim on his extremities, and seemed to be breathing with difficulty. Finally Stellworth could restrain himself no longer.

"Quite an active weekend, Bill," he put in before Doberman could frame an answer to Cinders' dangerous question. "A brief - an opera - did you also go to any art galleries?"

Stellworth was harking back, of course, to Doberman's mock phone conversation with Cinders. To Cinders, however, the comment was mere gibberish, and he waved Stellworth down with an impatient gesture.

With Stellworth duly suppressed, Cinders turned back to Doberman. Based on his experience taking depositions early in his career, he believed in first establishing a sound factual basis and then moving in to close quarters. He asked who had performed the opera's two lead roles.

Doberman shrugged even more expressively than the last time. Not knowing the names even of the lead characters, much less the singers who played them, he was still framing his answer (perhaps something like "you know, the one who sounds like Domingo") when he was rescued by a further interruption. Cinders' buzzer sounded, announcing an urgent phone call.

Compared to the conversion of wine into water or any similar occurrence, this event was hardly miraculous. Cinders typically received phone calls about every six minutes, at least half of them urgent. Yet Doberman greeted his salvation with no less emotion than Saul of Tarsus, and shot out the door, with a whispered promise to return, before Cinders could stop him. Only one dark cloud darkened his elation. He had caught a glance from Stellworth that made it quite clear that his hesitation had not gone unnoticed. Stellworth plainly suspected him of not attending the opera. This added to the desperate urgency of procuring the information as soon as possible.

Suddenly, again like Saul on the road to Damascus, Doberman was struck by a blinding insight. The only and obvious solution to his difficulties was to go and ask Gidget O'Malley about the opera.

Approaching Gidget was potentially a significant step, since it might require advancing his intimacy with her to the extent of explaining why Lyla would not talk. It was true enough, for all his protestations, that Doberman and Gidget had been exchanging hungry glances in recent weeks. He often found himself fantasizing about how she looked in black underwear or unsnapping a bikini top.

Gidget's attractiveness to Doberman had something of the exotic, much as a young boy from India might pique the jaded sensuality of an aging Roman emperor. Coming from a totally different background than Doberman and with radically different values, Gidget had none of the neuroses that Doberman was used to, although conceivably she might substitute a full set of her own.

She was a typical child of southern California. Years of ruthless cultural indoctrination, supplemented by a year of free psychotherapy through her community college's health plan and a stint at Esalen with a boyfriend, had imbued her with the belief that, deep down, each and every one of us is a warm, loving, caring human being, differing only in degrees of self-knowledge. All evidence to the contrary she dismissed, although not in these terms, as manifesting mere false consciousness. For example, at Ashby & Cinders, she thought that people schemed and feuded simply because they did not love themselves enough, and thus mistakenly feared that they needed money, power, or status to achieve self-validation.

If Gidget had been a close personal friend of Genghis Khan's, she likely would have told him that he was not in touch with his feelings, and must be very unhappy. More commonly, though, if any friend of Gidget manifested false consciousness, she would employ raillery rather than direct criticism.

On this particular morning, Gidget was straightening her bangs in a pocket mirror when Doberman approached. She smiled as their eyes met. "Bill, this is a surprise. I haven't been seeing you much lately."

"I just had a question I wanted to ask you. Make that two questions."

"What's the first?"

"I was wondering how you liked the opera last night."

"It was very sweet of Lyla to ask me. She took me by

surprise. I've been feeling like she's angry at me lately for I don't know what."

"Don't mind that. Lyla is very thoughtful - if nothing else. But what I really want to know is about the production."

Lyla shrugged. "Opera's not my line, Bill. I only went because I've never been to the opera. You wouldn't believe how often I looked at my watch."

Doberman snorkered - half-snort, half-snicker - to show he wasn't so staid as to disapprove. "If you want to know a secret, Gidget, I do the same thing. But my question is a little different. For reasons to complex to go into, I need to know about the production so that I can talk to a senior partner as if I had been there."

"Can't Lyla help you?"

"That," said Doberman, again milking the dramatic pause, "leads to my second question. I really need to talk to someone, and I was wondering if you were free for dinner."

Within minutes, everything was arranged. While Gidget had absorbed little of the opera, she remembered that the audience had been enthusiastic, even without Doberman to shout, as he was wont to on these occasions, a showy "Bravissimo!!" Even more importantly, she still had the program in her purse.

They agreed to a late dinner at the restaurant he had previously mentioned to Lyla. Although he had invited Gidget on impulse, Doberman was beginning to relish the mordant irony of using the very bribe scorned by Lyla to assist in the attempted seduction of the woman she feared the most, and whom she had virtually thrown at him through a series of tactical blunders.

While Doberman now felt certain that he would attempt to start a secret affair with Gidget, he was less certain that he would succeed. In part, his luck might turn on the obscure workings of Gidget's California ideology. On the one hand, Lyla might qualify, in Gidget's mind, as a friend, and friends might be a category that precluded the expression of warm and deep inner feelings towards their consorts. On the other hand, it might be that friends in southern California went to bed with each other's spouses and lovers all the time.

7. Ups and Downs

For the next six hours and thirty-seven minutes, as measured by Doberman's watch, everything went like clockwork. Crossley, having been urged to read Doberman's section of the brief with extra care and attention, studiously avoided looking at it until after lunch. While he was out to lunch, Doberman effected the substitution of documents without being noticed.

On the Cinders front, Doberman gave a triumphant performance. He had gleaned some information from the program about tenor Andrea Traversi and soprano Teresa Luga, and was ready to let fly. It appeared that she was a bit more prominent, but why not reverse the conventional wisdom? He was feeling sportive.

"Traversi was really good," he said. "Small but intense." (This was a guess but with decent circumstantial support.) "I'd say he smoldered dramatically. He could be a straight actor. The voice was fine. I know some people say it's a bit thin, but what do they want? A foghorn?

"As for Luga, you know what a big name she is, but frankly I was not impressed. Technically, I thought she was a bit crude.

57

And the more discerning members of the audience seemed to be with me on this one. The applause was loud, yes, but I thought a bit hollow."

Cinders watched him with a little half-smile. To Doberman, it would have been sweeter still if Stellworth could have witnessed this conversation, but he found the strength to bear this disappointment.

Even Lyla, as if sensing the danger of her position, made gestures of reconciliation. Doberman had thought that this would take at least forty-eight hours, and that he would have to make the first gesture. It turned out that the guileless Gidget, while keeping quiet about her dinner plans, had told Lyla that Doberman seemed upset about the morning's disagreement. Lyla had been impressed by this, since Doberman usually tended to inscrutable play-acting. She decided to forgive Doberman's cleverness in procuring information about the opera from Gidget.

Once she had decided to reconcile, Lyla decided to go all the way. She cornered Doberman in the hallway and started murmuring in his ear suggestions about the evening that, while obscene, were anatomically quite possible. From a scheduling standpoint, however, they were less feasible. Remembering his date with Gidget, Doberman explained that he still did not feel well but should be better by Wednesday.

Doberman's work also went better after the nightmarish weekend. The burden of the Barlow case had given him an excuse to farm out the most unpleasant parts of his docket. For about two hours, he took a nap in his office, with his door closed and his secretary instructed to intercept any visitors until she could wake him by using his buzzer. He billed this time to his most obnoxious deep-pocketed client - a last, vestigial accommodation to half-remembered law student pieties about practicing law in the public interest.

Doberman also treated himself to a forty-minute lunch with a friend from another law firm, sneaking a lowly domestic beer since no one from Ashby & Cinders was looking. He returned to the office in an almost mellow mood, ready for an interval of daydreaming about his future glory.

Beyond a doubt, he thought comfortably as he lay back in his armchair, he would make partner next month. Crossley could hardly veto everyone. As for the competition, Porter was hopeless and Stellworth not smart enough. Perhaps Doberman would even get an office like Crossley's when he made partner. He could see himself sitting back in it and making people squirm, just as he had always had to as a young associate.

Being a partner would hardly end the life of drudgery that Doberman had experienced as an associate. Junior partners are in some ways akin to senior galley slaves. The real power would have to wait for at least another ten years or so. Still, Doberman could hope to take fewer orders than as an associate, and to give more. There was also the sporting aspect: no matter what the prize, at least he would have won.

The first year or two of partnership would not actually bring more money. In fact, with the capital contribution that he would have to make for his partnership share and the miniscule number of "points" that would be attributed to him in dividing the law firm's earnings, he might even take a temporary paycut. In other respects, however, satisfaction would arrive immediately. There would be the beaten look in Stellworth's eyes when he left for another law firm, the new deference from associates and staff, and a relatively free hand in dealing with Lyla and Gidget. Partners, just like associates, were not supposed to frolic with the help, but in practice (this being before the era of sexual harassment suits) they were the legal world's 900 pound gorillas.

Doberman remembered the famous story about the partner in a leading New York law firm who had been having an affair with the wife of one of his associates. How nice the partner must have found it to be able to send the poor slob on frequent road trips, and of course to know in advance when he would be away. Eventually the poor slob, turned back at the airport by a canceled flight, had arrived back home unexpectedly and found his boss in bed with his wife. Naturally enough, the law firm refused to accept this sort of behavior. They had asked the associate to leave, on the ground that his continued presence there would be disruptive. He had lost his wife, too, although the firm did help him to get another (no doubt lower-paying and lower-status) job.

The section on assumption of risk, Doberman's latest salvo in the partnership campaign, really was not a bad job under the circumstances. And Crossley could not easily deny its merit if Barlow picked Ashby & Cinders to handle the rest of the case, or else more generally to take on a greater role in its regulatory and political battles in Washington. That was probably the real point here so far as the partners were concerned, since in all likelihood the Commission would stick to its asset sequestration order at this stage anyway. Even the outcome of this case, which thankfully would not be known until well after the partnership decision, was probably not as important as you had to tell yourself it was while working on the brief. Barlow would win or lose in the end, but its corporate life would go on. And even if it got socked with a heavy financial penalty, the blame might go to Nesson & Wesson for its handling of the fact-finding proceedings. Or, just as good, the blame would go to the Washington political-legal environment, where evidently you needed the best sharks in the pond just to be permitted to go on with your regular business.

In the Barlow case, therefore, Crossley must be playing for higher, or at least different, stakes than getting the asset sequestration order lifted. Thus, even if the FPHC's enforcement arm prevailed at this stage (surely the money bet), it might still turn out that Doberman's efforts had been of value to Crossley. Gratitude was unlikely to be a factor on partnership night, but it might be in Crossley's interest to give Doberman credit that would redound to himself. Crossley would no doubt be anxious to say that his team's outstanding efforts had helped win the firm a likelihood of extra business for which he should receive a share of the financial credit.

True, the credit could go to any or all of the three associates, and surely no more than one of them would be making partner. But Porter was not even worth a thought, at least until he switched from permanent press to freshly ironed shirts and got the stains out of his trousers. As for Stellworth, it was hard to feel too concerned after all the scams that Doberman had pulled off right in front of his nose over the last three days. There had been the mock phone call from Cinders, the Sunday night adventure in the library, the smuggling of the updated version of the brief, the scene in Cinders' office about the opera. . . . Stellworth had suspected much, and yet discovered nothing.

On the subject of the Sunday night adventure in the library, Doberman suddenly remembered a nagging thought, one that had been festering all day just below the conscious level. It related to *Tomcat Industries*, the case in which a motion for rehearing had been filed, but that he had been unable to check in the little red pamphlet. Rehearings were almost never granted, and published decisions almost never withdrawn, but still it would be good to know.

In another minute, Doberman was in the library, examining the red pamphlet by the main set of desks. Fumbling for the citation, he found the right page, ran his finger down a column, and finally caught sight of it. It contained a new page number listing, with a little black "r" next to it. "R" meant that the case he had relied upon and discussed in text, both the district court decision and the initial affirmance, had been reversed.

8. Sublimation

For a moment, Doberman's knees buckled under the weight of this disaster. *Tomcat Industries* was a critical case, at least in his account of things, and he had used it in several paragraphs to bolster a major side-argument. By now, the brief was out of his hands, and he would have difficulty getting it changed it even if willing to admit his mistake.

Quickly, he checked the advance sheets containing the revised opinion, and found it just as bad as he had feared. The Fourth Circuit had originally held that a warning to "check with your physician before using this product" sufficed to put people with high blood pressure on notice that they needed to inquire about heart attack risks. Nothing more specific was needed, even though the company knew about the heart attack problem and had left it off the packaging merely to avoid visual clutter. Doberman had used this to argue for assumption of risk with respect to Barlow's cigarettes, as a matter of law given the Surgeon General's warning.

What did the Surgeon General's warning say?, he had asked in his grandest rhetorical style. That cigarette smoking is dangerous to your health. On what ground was the

Commission now complaining about TDC? That smoking it is dangerous to your health. Surely the defendant stood on even stronger ground here than in *Tomcat Industries*, where the packaging had merely urged consultation, rather than forthrightly trumpeting a danger.

On rehearing, though, the Fourth Circuit explained that its initial decision had overlooked a crucial fact: that the heart attack risks came from a new additive to the diet pills, and therefore one that prior customers might reasonably have overlooked. True, upon its introduction the manufacturer had prominently placed the words "New and Improved!" on the packaging. The warning to consult was still there, and the list of active ingredients had been suitably modified. But, as the court so eloquently found – could the poets Donne or Shelley have said it any better? -

"We do not deem persuasive at this stage defendant's contention that each significant product modification, assuming prominently displayed notice of same, triggers as a matter of law duties of *de novo* inquiry on plaintiffs who must subsequently establish their reasonableness in these proceedings."

Hence, the Fourth Circuit now reversed the trial court's dismissal of the cause of action, and offered a new day in court for plaintiffs whose initial usage of the diet pills had preceded the introduction of the additive.

What did this imply for the Barlow case? It depended on whether trying a new brand of cigarette with TDC was more like taking a "New and Improved" version of the same old diet pills, in which case Barlow was in trouble, or more like trying a new product for the first time, in which case Barlow should do fine. Doberman's gut reaction was the former. New brands or not, everyone knew that the Surgeon General's warning was generic; it applied to all cigarettes. Barlow could not easily argue that consumers should have interpreted it as suggesting that they should consider anew the full set of relevant health risks every time they considered switching to a new brand of cigarette. Still, *Tomcat Industries* was just one case, from another circuit and not involving federal regulatory issues.

The possible consequences for Doberman personally of the Fourth Circuit's about-face were considerably starker than those for Barlow. Crossley would crucify him, one hoped in only a metaphorical sense, while Stellworth would plead for harsher punishment. Nesson & Wesson would have fun with Ashby & Cinders, and beyond doubt get to keep the case. Perhaps the firm would lose Barlow's business altogether, and Doberman would take the blame just before he came up for partner.

In the short run, there was at least the comfort that only Crossley was reviewing the document in house. He probably had not pulled Shepard's from the shelf since the day he made partner. The main threat, then, was Nesson & Wesson. A desperate plan began forming in Doberman's mind. Perhaps he could bribe someone in the mailroom to substitute a corrected copy for the one that Crossley had approved for general transmission. But even if this succeeded, and by now it was probably too late, it would mean that someone in the office who was bound to dislike his general demeanor towards male underlings would have the power to blackmail him. Maybe he could instead use a secretary. They tended to like him a lot better than the mailroom crew did. But on the other hand they were also more prone to gossip, or at least better situated to launch their gossip into general circulation.

Remembering the sword of Damocles, Doberman felt envious. At least Damocles had known that, if the thread snapped and the sword fell on his neck, his consciousness would be obliterated immediately. Doberman, by contrast, would have to live through several unpleasant meetings.

Rationally considered, the situation called for firming up his reconciliation with Lyla. Her father, being a name partner at Carp, Stone & Tyler, could be Doberman's last recourse if his actions were discovered and the story spread through the Washington legal community. Yet the prospect of rescue by Lyla was not an appealing one. Doberman could see himself being forced to marry her, with permanently diminished prestige and the knowledge that she could throw his failure in his face for as long as they both lived.

Thus, Doberman turned to the irrational viewpoint, the thought that he should live for today and let tomorrow take care of itself. Ennobled by his sense of suffering, or at least exalted by self-pity, he felt that he had earned the right to dinner with Gidget. Even if nothing came of it, he would at least enjoy her sympathy and regard.

Doberman was determined, however, that more than mere sympathy and regard would come from dinner. His many wounds and tribulations seemed, in his fevered imagination, to have sprouted mouths, each shouting that he must take Gidget to bed that very evening as compensation.

Though no novice at the art of seduction, Doberman knew that it would require one of his better performances. Conceivably, he might be hampered by the very urgency that impelled him to try. He always felt more convincing when saying things that he did not really believe.

Still, Doberman did not intend to let sincerity stop him. He had long been a master at retailing stories of hard knocks about his personal life. Beyond shrewdly measuring out the requisite doses of confidence and vulnerability, he knew how to hammer home the unstated theme that, depending on the audience, he was either Born Under a Bad Star or else Too Good.

Doberman well remembered the effect on Lyla – two parts Too Good to one Bad Star - when first he told her about his parents' divorce. Knowing that this would be a sure-fire topic given her own family history, he had made certain to get full value. Not that this was difficult; the material was pretty good. He gave first billing to Dad, morose since his business (a chain of hardware stores) had failed when Bill was nine, and working long hours for a former competitor just to keep some rudiments of the family's former standard of living. Second billing went to Mom, who probably never had liked staying home and now was drinking a fair amount and hiding it less. Probably at around this time she had started an affair (previously Dad's exclusive province). Brother Patrick he acknowledged but played down as tending by his very presence to dilute the narrative impact of A Boy Alone. Still, the punchline of expressing deliberately unrealistic expectations of himself as a nine to fourteen year old while the drama played out was effective, Patrick or no.

"I could have helped them somehow," he told her. "Instead of acting out with my brother and making things worse. I shouldn't have complained so much about getting less of everything, like vacations and new clothes. Even though it affected my status at school. Taken an after-school job. I don't know – just been less sarcastic with them."

These regrets were not very sincere - Doberman had long since written off his parents, and concluded that he must be the family changeling, its sole white sheep - but Lyla had eaten it up, glad to get a peek behind the mask that she didn't yet realize was just another mask. With Gidget, however, his pitch would have to be more nuanced. If Lyla was a sucker for the fist-pumping Rocky-movie strategy, then Gidget called for something along the lines of Cary Grant mixed with Eddie Van Halen.

When Doberman arrived at the restaurant, Gidget was waiting for him. She was seated at a table in a dark corner, her auburn hair and full face framed in candlelight, sipping a gin and tonic.

"Pretty fancy place," she said as he sat down.

"Good food, too."

"It's a bit steep for my budget."

"Don't worry about that. It's my treat."

"Really."

"It's my pleasure. Call it redistribution of wealth."

Doberman now carefully kept the conversation light. A hunter never flushes out the quarry too soon.

Gidget as well was playing coy. She accepted his food and wine recommendations without seeming to notice the accompanying show of virtuosity. If it matters to you that's fine, she seemed to be saying. Conversation lagged until the wine arrived. By the time the appetizers came, they were nearly through the first bottle, and Gidget was ready to talk business.

Doberman had just been waxing sportive about what various of the firm's partners must have been like when they were children, when she broke in.

"Bill, I wanted to settle something. Is this a date?"

The sudden change of topic was a warning sign; he might be starting to bore her. Doberman realized that he had been losing track of the agenda.

"Let's talk about that later."

"Okay."

"And I'm sorry about the shop talk."

"That's okay."

"I'd really like to forget about office things for now."

He steered the conversation to their childhoods, looking for common threads. It turned out that she also had a parent who drank too much, although for her it was the father. Her parents were still married, but hardly talked to each other now. Mother had raised five children without a lot of help – Gidget was the third - and now didn't know what to do with herself. Gidget did not want to end up like her.

"Is that why you moved to Washington?" he asked.

"Not really. Maybe on some level. Actually, I'd call it either wanderlust or getting dumped."

"*You* got dumped? That I can't believe."

"Oh, but you should believe it."

The sad story followed. For about five years, starting when

she was still in school, she had dated a man, also named Bill, who was twelve years older than her. He was pretty amazing, or at least he had seemed to be at the time. He was successful in business but not serious about it, took enjoying himself seriously, and had a spiritual side. He knew all kinds of things, from the history of transcendental meditation to where to go at night in Tijuana to how to fix a fan belt.

Then one day, while Gidget was at work but he was giving himself a day off at the beach, he had met someone.

"Another woman?" Doberman superfluously asked.

"A seventeen year old. Supposed to be a classic blonde bunny, and probably as naïve as I was when I met him."

Just like that, he took up with the girl, spending marathon sessions with her in motel bedrooms to lessen the chance that her parents would interfere. At least, so Gidget had heard. He had not even given her a call.

"How did he tell you, then?"

"He didn't. That same day, he was supposed to meet me when I got off work, and he never showed up. I couldn't get him on the phone, and he never called me back. At first I thought he must be injured or dead or something. I even called the hospital. A couple of days later I heard about it from some people who saw him with her."

"Wow. That must have been tough."

Gidget smiled but didn't say anything.

"So you just picked up and moved to Washington?"

"Not right away. This whole thing was about a year ago."

"And you've been here for three months."

"Actually four. I was thinking of just temping, but they asked me to stay here and I figured why not."

"I'm glad you did."

Another smile. "Well, thank you, Mr. Doberman."

This might be another warning signal. Don't press things too soon; remember that listening is the best aphrodisiac.

"What did you do right after he disappeared on you?"

"Nothing. When I finally knew what had happened, I got really drunk, but just once. I don't like the hangovers any more, you know?"

Doberman gave a short, and he hoped sage, nod. "That's the advantage to getting stoned."

"*You* get stoned!?"

He had meant to surprise her, but not quite that much. "I used to. Mainly in college. Just every now and then. But let's get back to your breakup. What did you do" - here a trained litigator's rephrasing of the question - "in the period right after this guy disappeared on you?"

"Really absolutely nothing. I'd go to work and go home. I saw my family more than usual, but that was even more depressing. My friends took me out a lot, which was nice."

Your lips are so full and soft, he was thinking. In this light your eyes seem darker brown, less hazel.

"And after a while you just couldn't take it any more?"

Gidget frowned. Evidently this way of putting it was either too pathetic for her or else too melodramatic. Maybe both. "I just didn't see the point to staying there any longer. It was time for something new."

"Why Washington?"

"No reason. A girlfriend wanted to see the sights here, the Capital and all that. I decided to come along, then I ended up driving her after we flipped a coin. I thought at the time, maybe this is telling me something. Then we were in Alexandria, I liked it okay there, and I saw a sign for furnished rental apartments, month to month. I figured why not."

"And here you are."

"And here I am."

"You'll laugh at me again if I say I'm glad."

"You could give it a try if you like. But you're probably right."

This marked the end of a movement. Doberman was

wondering if he should open a new line of inquiry or start his turn at sharing personal history, but she spoke up first.

"I asked you something earlier, you know."

"Yes, is this a date. I guess I owe you an answer." He waited a beat. "Okay, I'll take the plunge. Yes. On the assumption you're leaving it up to me."

"What about Lyla?"

Doberman gestured expressively with his hands and eyebrows. "Lyla is Lyla."

"What does that mean?"

"I don't know what she wants." This line was always good for starters. In fact, however, Doberman thought he knew what Lyla wanted: a ring for her finger and a yoke around his neck.

"You're having a fight?"

"It's more than that. Well we are, but just the usual. It's always my fault. No, I mean that, I'm not being sarcastic. I just give in and give in to her, trying to be supportive because she needs it. Then at some point I get fed up. Without any warning, I just want something my own way. It's usually just a tiny little thing. Oops, maybe this time I am being sarcastic. Then she gets mad."

This is pretty creative, he thought. It's a good thing she hasn't been questioning other witnesses. Also, that she works on the tenth floor, out of the way.

"Have you ever thought about relationship counseling?" she asked.

"I, she, she's against it." As indeed Lyla would have been, thinking counseling was for crazy people. But of course, just think about the effect on his standing at the office if he went to counseling, even couples counseling, and people found out about it.

Quickly he pressed on. What concerned him was this attitude of Lyla's and also, well, the pattern. The way they were trapped right now and just not working on it. He had wanted to resolve some things, but at a certain point you could just start feeling defeatist.

Gidget was leaning forward slightly, her eyes on his and her lips - well, from the looks of things maybe they, too, would soon be on his. Doberman grew sufficiently encouraged to take his two main themes so far, celebratory self-criticism and put-downs of Lyla masked as compassion, and begin subtly mixing in a third. The time had come, he realized, for code words delivering sexual sub-texts with an air of sensitivity.

Thus, when he said "I feel imprisoned," he knew it sounded much better than a direct statement that he craved more sexual variety.

Then there was "I'm not sure I'm being fair to her." This meant that Lyla had no chance of landing him anyway, so Gidget should not feel bad about getting in the way.

"I don't want to hurt her," meant that any relationship with Gidget would have to be conducted secretly.

"I need to find out how I really feel about her" suggested that an affair with Gidget would actually help Lyla, by speeding the process of decision. Then came the masterful "I wish I knew what I want." What woman could resist the challenge to show that what he wanted was her? To Gidget, the challenge was even stronger, her ideology commanding her to put people in touch with their feelings even if she remained unsure of her own.

At long last, Doberman decided there was nothing more to belabor. A jazz combo was playing decorously in the background, and he suggested to Gidget that they dance. They discovered that, while neither knew many steps, they were able to keep time well together. At first he held her out away from his body, his elbows slightly bent as he grasped her hands or gingerly held her waist or shoulder, but gradually he reeled her in.

"You're a good dancer," Gidget murmured, snuggling comfortably against him.

"You're a good kisser," she whispered later. And, observing his technique with her clothing, she suggested that he must have a lot of parties Lyla did not know about. This cynicism notwithstanding, she showed no second thoughts once the decision had been made and, when not enthusiastically straining in his arms, was sleeping trustfully with her head against his shoulder.

9. Another Day

The next morning, the Sun, showing little sense of romance, rose at precisely the expected time. Doberman and Gidget still were cradled together, she chattering about the pizza in Washington while he stroked her haunches and agonized about his erroneous case citation. For once, his dynamic man of action mode was in abeyance.

Suddenly she looked at the clock and squealed: "Eight o'clock! I have to leave!"

Fresh clothes and her curling iron and everything were back in Alexandria. She would have to call in late as it was, and she could not stay to shower with him and have breakfast, although he was sweet to suggest it.

In other households, the arrival of morning was far more welcome. Crossley had been awake since four-thirty, counting as he lay in bed the minutes until he could get up and begin preparations to escape to his big, empty office. He had always felt ambivalent about sharing his bed with another person, leaving aside those increasingly infrequent moments of lust. Spouses should be colleagues, he thought, and have a closer, more trusting bond than law firm partners (except maybe in a two-man office), but why did they have to be right on top of each other all the time?

On this particular morning, Crossley's anxiety to leave was even greater than usual, lest Anne insist on talking to him about last night. Again the April weather had let him down, permitting her brother Wayne to come over with wife and son for a backyard cookout.

Even just as a general matter, Crossley hated cookouts. The charcoal would never stay lit for him, or at least it liked to wait for someone else to step in and take the credit. Wayne it seemed to like just fine, maybe because he remembered about opening the grate.

But the problem wasn't just cookouts, and it wasn't even really Wayne. Of Wayne, Crossley thought charitably enough: I could take him or leave him. There was, to be sure, the detectable hint of condescension when something like this grill problem happened. Like that time on vacation a couple of summers ago when Crossley had almost backed them all into a ditch. There really had been no way of seeing the ditch from the driver's seat, but Wayne didn't seem to understand this. One often got the faintly conveyed sense from him that Anne's first husband had been, well, maybe more of a man. Yet Wayne was civil enough, really, and also he earned a lower income than Crossley.

But Wayne, Junior ... now we were talking about some nasty human material. Sooner or later the Mob, or maybe the Cali drug cartel, was bound to hear about Wayne, Junior. They would certainly offer him a job, at least if they were hiring overweight nine year olds.

Only last summer he hit me in the shoulder with a beebee gun, Crossley recalled. No wonder I was so edgy last night seeing him with a water gun. The threats were credible, darn it.

The worst the boy had actually done at the cookout was tell on Crossley for cursing in front of him when the charcoal wouldn't light. But this had been bad enough. "Peter said fuck! Peter said fuck!" he had reported delightedly, leaving Crossley to face reprimands from both Anne and her sister, the boy's mother. As if one could possibly, just through words the boy no doubt used all the time anyway, exert a bad influence on this sort of human garbage.

Anne was probably going to suggest some sort of outing so Crossley could get more comfortable with Wayne, Junior. What a brilliant idea. Crossley keenly remembered the time last summer when he had taken the boy miniature golfing, all by himself since Anne at the last minute had gotten an important phone call and been forced to back out of the venture. Rather than be dumbly grateful, Wayne, Junior had loudly accused him of cheating, right in front of a dozen people waiting for their turns somewhere on the back nine. Having to play sports was bad enough without someone watching your every move.

Lowell Stellworth, as he sat with his wife at breakfast, was scarcely less anxious than Crossley to leave for work this morning. Stellworth had slept no more than the others on Monday night, brooding about Doberman's Houdini-like capacity to escape the consequences of crime. Now he was finding it difficult to take the proper interest in Sarah's account of her latest squabble with the other local Arts Council volunteers. He barely could manage to provide on cue the responses dictated by inflexible family tradition.

"And Netta agreed with me," she was telling him.

"Oh, how lovely."

"She said absolutely, at the cocktail reception we don't want those little toasted franks in rolls. Lowell, can you imagine, caviar and toasted franks--"

"Oh, how horrid."

"And I said to Dorothy, bring whatever you want, whether it's frankfurters or toasted fiddlesticks, but I'm going to

Ardsley's for some canapes, even if I have to pay for them myself."

"Oh, how lovely."

"Lowell! Why should I have to pay for them?"

The approach of departure time also beckoned welcomingly to Porter as he sat at breakfast. Janet, noticing that he seemed unusually glum even by his standards, was trying to have a serious conversation about the reasons for his certainty that he would never make partner at Ashby & Cinders. Brian the five year old and Ted the three year old plainly agreed with him, however - no doubt for their own distinct reasons - that this was not a well-chosen use of the family's only regular mealtime together.

The boys also disagreed that it was mealtime, but that was another matter. Brian was actually putting on his shirt, despite having been asked only twice, because he wanted to watch a video before Mom and Ted took him to kindergarten. Ted had seized the opportunity to tackle Brian while the shirt was over his eyes, leading to howls and kicks along with threats of retribution - "Ted can't play with my fire trucks any more!" - "MY fire trucks!" - until, as swiftly as they had started, they subsided to work on a fire-fighting set-up together.

Porter got up to toast a couple of Pop Tarts for them, on the off-chance that their tastes had not changed radically over the last twenty-four hours (he had forgotten to ask about their dinner). Janet raised her hand for him to stop. This was her opportunity to have a quiet talk with him, and she meant to take it.

"You work hard, Arnold. You're smart. You're nice. You do everything they tell you. Why should there be any question that you'll make partner?"

"They don't look at it that way. It's all politics."

"Daddy, what's politics?"

It was amazing that Brian had heard them. He had been starting to lecture Ted about the Great Chicago Fire. Mrs.

O'Leary's cow was the one who did it because she (Mrs. O'Leary or the cow?) wasn't being careful.

"Politics is when grown-ups vote for people, like to be the President. Or when they - "

"Are you running for President, Daddy?"

"No, but there's going to be a vote at my office that I want to win, and that's politics too."

"Are you going to win?"

Janet cut in. "We don't know. Sometimes in politics people aren't fair to other people, and that's what Daddy and I are talking about right now."

They had lost him, however, and Janet got back down to business.

"Even if it's politics, don't be so gee-ell-oh-oh" - she waved her hand to start again - "so dee-oh-double-u-en about it. You never have fights with anyone. You don't have any enemies."

"Mommy, can I have a blue Pop Tart?" It was Brian again.

"Red for me!" sang Ted.

Porter jumped up to fill their orders, but Janet followed him into the kitchen, so he had to answer.

"Everyone's my enemy. Certainly, no one's my friend."

"That's so negative."

"I'm trying. Will you give me a chance?"

Immediately he felt bad about himself for being so brusque with her. You could argue that Janet worked harder than he did, all things considered, even if her paycheck was only for thirty hours a week.

It was this stifling atmosphere of faith and trust in him that made him so testy, with the partnership verdict approaching. At the office he almost relished the daily punishment, intermingled with long periods that were at least calm and quiet. But at home he just felt guilty about things, or else that the boys were stretching his nerves thin with their clamor.

Porter left, accordingly, if not with a song on his lips, then at least with a quickened step.

By 9:24 in the morning - according to the lawyers' time sheets, which divided each hour, for billing purposes, into ten six-minute segments - all members of the Barlow Industries brief-writing team had arrived at the office. The next few hours were uneventful, but at 1:06 Crossley got the client's verdict: thumb squarely to the side, not up or down. Nesson & Wesson would still officially be filing tomorrow's brief. But they would be cutting and pasting in substantial material from the Ashby & Cinders brief in close consultation with Barlow's in-house attorneys. Ashby & Cinders would be listed on brief as "of counsel." At the reply brief stage in about five weeks, both firms would play a role, with Nesson & Wesson still officially in the lead but the real power relationship as yet unsettled. Nesson & Wesson might be anywhere from mere figureheads to actually running the show again. After that, for any subsequent FPHC proceedings or district court litigation, who knew? Crossley instructed his secretary to tell his underlings what was known through the reply brief stage.

Doberman now had reason to hope that the ill-cited case would just go away. Conceivably Nesson & Wesson, seeking to strengthen its position, would tell Barlow about finding an egregious error in the A & C brief, but this seemed unlikely and in any case there was nothing he could do about it.

With the crisis at least temporarily in abeyance, Doberman turned to the Lyla issue. Gidget must have arrived by some point in the mid-morning, but had dutifully avoided contacting him in any way. It was important that he call Lyla and find out how she was doing - he should probably have done this hours ago - particularly in light of her surprising failure to call him at home the previous evening.

It turned out that Lyla had called in sick. Doberman immediately phoned her at home, and was annoyed to hear Doris answer.

"Do you always call sick people when they're sleeping?" she asked in her most peevish tone.

"I'm very sorry. Is Lyla sleeping?"

"Actually, no. But she easily might have been."

"Is it all right if I speak to her?"

Doris probably did not think it was all right, but she relinquished the telephone anyway.

"Hi, honey," Lyla's voice floated over the wire. She seemed in almost impossibly good humor, given that she generally considered illness a personal insult.

"Are you okay?" Doberman asked her.

"Not really. But do you remember the time I pulled a muscle in my stomach from too much Nautilus?"

Doberman remembered it well. Lyla had taken this injury with all the equanimity that Castro must have lavished on the Bay of Pigs invasion. "Is it another muscle injury? I thought you were sick."

"I am sick. Who said I'm not sick? But do you remember those aspirins laced with codeine that they gave me so it wouldn't hurt so much? I had a few left over."

A drugged Lyla, obviously, was a happy Lyla. Doberman wondered if any narcotics can dull suspicion as effectively as pain.

It turned out that Lyla had nothing more serious than tonsillitis. Her fever had reached high levels on Monday night, while Doberman was experiencing a fever of a different kind, but now she was barely over 100. She had been told she should recover within forty-eight hours.

Doberman's expression of relief upon hearing this was entirely sincere. Among other things, it meant forty-eight hours of free play with Gidget, and forty-eight hours before any decisions would have to be made. In a burst of benevolence, mingled with pragmatism, Doberman promised to stop by after work, and to bring anything that Lyla thought she might need. He would stay as long as she wanted, making his best

Florence Nightingale-style show of indifference to his own personal health and safety, and then, if all went well, would leave for an assignation with Gidget. Doberman had little fear of getting sick from Lyla, even if he did spend an hour or two sharing her oxygen, as he firmly believed that he was physically invulnerable.

With Lyla taken care of, Doberman turned back to the Barlow case. He phoned Crossley's secretary, determined that neither Stellworth nor Porter had stopped by yet, and decided to pay a triumphal visit himself. A bit of favorable re-contexting of events was needed, to make sure Crossley was adopting the right perspective.

Bursting in unannounced, Doberman saw Crossley furtively shove the New York Times beneath a stack of papers, as if afraid to be seen shirking work even by an associate. Crossley, seeing from Doberman's expression that he had been detected, grinned unpleasantly.

"Is there something I can do for you, Bill? Or did you just come by to admire my office again?"

"I was just wondering how you score the Barlow matter at this point."

Crossley shrugged.

"I think it's a total victory!" Doberman said. "Those other guys should pay us by the word for everything they take from our brief."

"It could have been worse," Crossley conceded. "Of course, if you guys had finished on Sunday, I would have had the chance to refine it a little more. Then maybe we'd have the case outright."

Doberman saw that there was no more to gain here, and headed off to needle Stellworth. He burst in asking "Have you heard the good news?" This was understood by both as an insult, insinuating as it did that Stellworth would not have been informed of things as promptly.

Stellworth winced as usual upon noticing Doberman's arrival.

"Is that what you call it," he said in a kind of drawl. Tit for tat; he was suggesting that Doberman must have too lax a definition of success.

"Oh, you mean you're worried that we're still just of counsel. Peter Crossley and I just worked it all out. It's pure face-saving for Nesson, or really for whoever at Barlow told senior management to hire those guys. Obviously they were never going to change officially unless it got them an extension. They don't want the Commission to think they're desperate."

"You just figured this out?"

"But here's the key. Ours was the better brief, and Barlow is going to make Nesson use ours a lot. So we scored. Peter thinks assumption of risk is what put us over the top."

"Did he," said Stellworth in his driest tone. As if Crossley would ever praise an associate to his face.

Stellworth then fell pointedly silent and looked back down, hoping that Doberman would take the hint and leave, but to no avail.

"Peter is really sanguine. He even said he'd like to bet money that assumption of risk ends up winning the case for us. Maybe even next month through a dismissal after the reply briefs. Short and sweet."

Stellworth still had nothing to say.

"He has hopes for jurisdiction, too, but he said he just wishes it had fallen into place a bit better."

Stellworth could at least believe that Doberman had advanced this view. "Would you mind if I do a little work now?" he asked. "Just in case we haven't won the case yet."

When Doberman left, however, Stellworth found that he was having trouble concentrating. It was just too much for Doberman to seize the juiciest topic and then go around boasting about it. Thinking back on how Doberman had appropriated assumption of risk, Stellworth had a sudden inspiration.

At a critical moment in the discussion among the three associates, Doberman had seemed to receive a phone call from Cinders. During this phone call, Doberman had apparently been ordered to do assumption of risk, purportedly so he would have time to visit an art gallery. Doberman had subsequently almost denied the conversation, and certainly had not had time to go to an art gallery during the weekend, especially if he had gone to the opera.

What was more, Cinders had not responded to Stellworth's mention of art galleries during the previous morning's conversation about the opera. Stellworth decided that he would go to Cinders, and find out once and for all if Doberman had simply invented the conversation.

To Stellworth at certain moments, no less than to Doberman, to think was to act. Almost immediately, he was in Cinders' office. The great man was on the telephone, but Stellworth waited patiently. At length his chance came.

"Mr. Cinders, I'm sorry to bother you," he started, and Cinders nodded as if Stellworth was right to be sorry.

"A question has arisen about something. It's related to work, but also to - to some things other than work that you, and I, and others, like to think about in our spare time, that is, when we have spare time, of course."

Cinders nodded again, this time to acknowledge that he, at least, had reached the stage at which concerns other than narrowly professional ones were appropriate.

"I was wondering, at any rate, if it was true, as I have heard, that you gave Bill Doberman tickets to the opera last weekend."

"Yes, I did. And a very fine job he did about it. The upshot before much longer could be that I land a new - oh, say mid-sized - client."

This was gall and wormwood to Stellworth, but still he

persisted. "You didn't ask him to go to an art gallery over the weekend, then?"

"No. Didn't you hear me? I asked him to go to the opera."

"He has been telling people that you invited him to an art gallery."

"Why in the hell would he say that? It was the opera."

Just as Stellworth started trying to explain the circumstances, Cinders' buzzer sounded. Cinders waved Stellworth down impatiently, said "Now, if you'll excuse me," and picked up the telephone.

Stellworth realized that he could stay no longer without seriously provoking Cinders. Still, disturbing though it was to have irritated a name partner, he felt that he had made some progress. The art gallery story had been definitively rebutted. He considered complaining directly to Crossley, but decided that it would be better to start with Porter. That way, he could make sure of his supporting witness to the conversation, and leave Doberman in the position of having to argue against the overwhelming weight of the evidence.

Stellworth found Porter staring at the ceiling. For a moment, neither one spoke. Stellworth felt embarrassed, wondering how to begin and regretting the twenty minutes since his last cup of coffee.

Porter, for his part, was too surprised by Stellworth's visit to heed the social amenities. Stellworth was the sort of man who, when not getting hoity-toity with the hoi polloi, would just as soon be hobnobbing with the Nob Hill aristocracy. He did not generally socialize with other associates, or even speak to them beyond the professionally unavoidable.

In halting tones, half-strangled by passion, Stellworth explained the reason for his visit. He had caught Doberman - the way he hissed the name, it was unnecessary to add "that fiend" - in an outright lie. Doberman had pretended to receive a phone call from Cinders just so that he could steal assumption of risk from Porter, who - surely he remembered - had previously laid claim to it. Now, with Cinders' absolute denial that any such conversation had taken place, all that was needed was Porter's corroborating evidence in order to convict Doberman of - Stellworth drew the words out slowly, with relish - "a most uncollegial course of conduct."

Porter heard him out patiently and with amazement. Despite understanding the high stakes for which the partnership war was being fought, it had never occurred to him that anyone would do something like this. Perhaps it was simply a failure of imagination. Yet Porter thought of Doberman's act as displaying a lack, not so much of decency as proportion. He could think of circumstances in which he himself might do something similar - say, to save Ted from being hit by a bus (although it seemed unlikely that lying about a phone call would help with that), or maybe to escape wrongful conviction for murder. But just to switch sections on a brief? Just one of a million tasks during the six years they were being considered for partnership, even if it was situated rather close to the finish line?

Still, Porter refused to help Stellworth take counter-measures. "Isn't it punishment enough that Bill's the type of person who would do something like that?"

"Punishment enough?!?" demanded Stellworth. "What punishment? Do you want him to make partner next month?"

"That's not my decision." And, far from agreeing to tattle, Porter promised amnesia about the art gallery conversation if Stellworth made it into a public issue.

The livid Stellworth thought this tantamount to treason. Was Porter just a cynical wage-slave, performing his stipulated duties with no sense of a higher mission? Didn't he grasp the importance, for the sake of Ashby & Cinders, of making sure that Stellworth, rather than Doberman, would be the one to beat him out for partner? A cutting remark was most in order here, and Stellworth felt bitter enough to stoop to sarcasm, or even, despite its cheapness, to irony. Unable to think of anything, however, he withdrew.

Doberman, meanwhile, was reaping the fruits of Stellworth's tactless interrogation of Cinders. Shortly after the futile visit, Cinders had received a phone call informing him that an important Japanese client was in town and would be available for dinner. The best thing to do, Cinders considered, would be to take him to a Japanese restaurant, in order to make him feel right at home. Unfortunately, however, Cinders distrusted sushi, fearing that it might have worms, and preferred not risking that this become known. A Chinese restaurant, then, was the next best thing. As a simple matter of geography, China was pretty close to Japan.

There was only one problem. Having resolutely pursued a career as a European, and above all, a French, restaurant snob, Cinders did not know where a good Chinese restaurant could be found in Washington. In particular, he did not know any that were sufficiently expensive.

Stellworth was the natural Chinese restaurant authority among the associates, having traveled to China on business and brought back a lithograph for his office. After the nonsense about the art gallery, however, Cinders found himself wondering if Stellworth was really the sort of nice young man he wanted for the job of flunky and cultural confidant. Cinders thought he might prefer someone more frothily deferential, someone more like, well, Doberman.

Cinders banged his buzzer to alert his secretary, and within thirty seconds the young man was standing in his office. Doberman smirked throughout Cinders' ponderous summation of the circumstances, knowing that Stellworth was the natural person to consult on this matter. Finally he directed Cinders to the most expensive Chinese restaurant he knew.

"You'll love this place. Slow service, but very attentive,

and dinner for two should cost at least $100, so he'll know it's a class place."

"Excellent."

Doberman decided to probe a little further into the circumstances surrounding Cinders' question. "Have you thought of asking Stellworth? He's supposed to be quite an expert on the subject." Ordinarily, only hot tongs could have drawn this admission from him.

"Stellworth - bah. That young man has to calm down."

Doberman looked wisely at Cinders. Then he looked down for a moment, as if deep in thought, raised his eyes to meet Cinders' again, and nodded sagely, his hand stroking his chin. "Just immaturity," he said. "I've tried to help him, but these things take time."

10. Another Night

That evening on the early side, Doberman dropped by Lyla's apartment. He found his inamorata lying restlessly in her bedroom. Doris herself, stopping her own bustling to wait for Doberman's departure, leaned against the wall and glared at him suspiciously.

"Don't go near her," Doris commented, "and don't stay too late. She's very sick."

Doberman did not intend to stay very late in any case. He expected Gidget at his apartment in about two hours. Still, anxious not to stint on the warm-up routine, he smiled fondly and produced twelve long-stemmed red roses from inside his coat, with the air of a magician performing a conjuring trick.

"I brought you these," he said to Lyla, rather redundantly, since she could hardly have thought that he found them beneath the carpet.

"Thanks," she said listlessly. "Mother, get a vase."

Ordinarily, Lyla reacted to flowers more fervidly. She liked them almost as much as Cinders liked new clients. Obviously, then, the codeine binge had ended, and she was feeling considerably worse.

"So you have tonsillitis," Doberman mused, still anxious to win a response. "I thought only kids got that."

"I didn't make it up."

"You never had your tonsils removed?"

"If I had, I probably wouldn't have tonsillitis."

"You really should have that taken care of. It's not bad - for a few days afterwards they give you nothing but ice cream."

Too late, Doberman remembered that ice cream was a sensitive subject with Lyla. She loved it, but her weight maintenance program hated it, particularly after the last week, when she had learned that she was half a pound over her target weight.

Her reply, under the circumstances, was comparatively mild. "Don't mention food. Mother's been force-feeding me with tea and Jello all day."

Doberman shrugged and smiled. "What would you like to talk about?"

"Well, for one thing, you could ask me how I'm feeling."

"How are you feeling?"

"Don't ask. My fever's back over 101, and I feel terrible. Whenever I swallow, it feels like I have a knife in my throat - "

"Perhaps you shouldn't swallow."

"- but for some reason I have to swallow every two seconds." She winced as she swallowed again.

Doris returned, with the roses ensconced in a vase – bright red background with a flower pattern engraved on the side – that seemed to have been chosen to in order to mute his offering. She pushed the vase onto the back corner of the dresser, as far from the light as possible. Her presence helped to make the conversation, even such as it was, begin to languish still more. So Doberman, after a few pleasantries on the subject of bacterial versus viral illnesses, headed out, sighing in relief once the door was closed.

Returning home with more than an hour to waste before

Gidget's scheduled arrival, Doberman found that he had a lot to think about. As a student of human nature, albeit from an intensely practical perspective, he knew what to make of Lyla's peevishness whenever she was feeling less than physically and emotionally perfect. He suspected that it is when an individual is sick, tired, hurt, or desperate that the mask comes off. And his fondness for wearing a mask on every occasion in no way lessened his interest in seeing what lay behind everyone else's.

Maybe this was a bit unfair to Lyla. It was not as if she had some real inner core of peevishness, going deeper than anything else, with the times when she was nice being simply for show. Better to think of it in terms of Pavlov's dogs. Give her something she liked and she was nice. Give her something she hated and she was not so nice. It wasn't like you were peeling away an onion. Probably the same was true of most people.

Nonetheless, Doberman could feel a touch of mute horror as he reflected on some aspects of what it might be like if he were married to Lyla. He could see her getting sick, expelling him from the bedroom, and summoning her mother to be a visitor until the crisis was over. He would be reduced to the status of a bondservant, fetching damp facecloths for her brow and running to the pharmacy to pick up prescriptions.

Luckily, she did not get sick often. Yet he found himself wondering why he had stayed with her for so long. One reason was sexual convenience given his busy schedule, but now Gidget was available. And anyway, he had never found it that hard to meet women given any reasonable opportunities. At least, in his twenties it had been pretty easy, and even at thirty-one he could see no reason to think that he had lost his touch just yet.

Obviously, he must really like the challenge that Lyla presented. He never felt securely dominant over her, even though she wanted to marry him. And when she was in good spirits, she could be so enthrallingly appreciative that it was difficult to compare anyone else.

Lyla viewed him, at the best of times, as the clever, passionate, Machiavellian hero of a show like *Dallas* or *Dynasty*. She would listen tirelessly to his tales of law firm intrigue, remembering every detail and rooting for him vigorously. The feeling of being appreciated like this, followed by intervals of petty bickering, always left Doberman thirsting for more. It was like being a standup comic, hooked on making people laugh, or else a heroin addict.

With Gidget, perhaps Doberman could cure his addiction, or at least switch to Methadone. Determined to treat her in style, he called a fancy restaurant for reservations, ran out to get a bottle of white wine that he could chill in time for after dinner as well as a pack of condoms, and took an extra shower with scented soap.

Soon Gidget arrived, carrying an overnight bag and dressed in tight faded jeans and a pink Venice Beach T-shirt with no bra. Enticing though she looked, Doberman was disappointed.

"You look very nice," he told her, "but I probably should have said something. I've made reservations at Dominique's, and we don't have much time."

"Dominique's? Is that the place where they serve stuff like rattlesnake?"

"That's right. Very good food, though, and we should be just in time for the prix fixe menu. I hope they don't mind your T-shirt and jeans; it's kind of a dressy place."

Gidget pouted. "Do we have to go to a fancy restaurant?"

"I thought it would be nice. What do you have in the overnight bag? A skirt?"

"Well yeah, but I was thinking we could do something more casual."

Doberman was stunned. Most of the women he had

sought out in his Washington years liked to spend his money in fancy restaurants. Whether they expected to enjoy the food or not, they took it as a sign of genuine interest if not good intentions.

"What would you rather do?" he asked.

"Let's just have a party."

"A party? What do you mean? Who can we invite at this hour?"

"I was thinking of a private party."

Doberman was silent, baffled by the challenge to his plans.

"No need to look so hurt about it," Gidget said, reaching out to touch his arm. "Did you make any party preparations for just the two of us?"

He thought he wouldn't mention the condoms. "Well, I did get a bottle of wine on the way home."

"Now, that's the type of preparation I like."

It turned out that Gidget's favorite type of party involved simply having pizza delivered, getting drunk in front of the television, retiring to the bedroom, and making love to the sound of Vivaldi or Billy Joel. No DJs, fancy hors d'oeuvres, or of course guests as he had thought were associated with using the word. Much though Doberman liked to control all planning within a five-mile radius of his person, he could see the merits of this type of party .

In the morning, as they held each other and waited for the alarm clock to sound, he began telling her about his latest triumphs with Cinders. Unfortunately, not having heard the earlier history of his feud with Stellworth, she needed a lot of side-explanations in order to grasp the context. Once she understood, she was surprised that he attached so much importance to Cinders' friendly gesture about the Chinese restaurant.

"Why even care about those things?" she asked him. "Just

do what you have to during the day, then go home and do what you want to, and you'll probably be much happier."

"You don't understand. Stellworth spends twenty-four hours a day scheming and plotting against me."

"That's his problem. Let him go gray worrying."

Doberman did not think that he was worrying too much. His actions towards Stellworth struck him, in every respect, as the very pinnacle of rationality. This hardly seemed the right time to argue, however. Better to work on getting her in the mood for a leisurely, soapy hot shower.

Life is not fair, Jimmy Carter had in recent memory remarked, and if Porter had known about Doberman's Tuesday night in contrast to his own, he might have felt this all the more strongly. He had to work until 9 o'clock, completing a noisome 50-state review memo on water pollution ordinances. The conversation with Stellworth had been bothering him all evening, and he planned to tell Janet about it as soon as he got home.

By the time he put his key in the lock, it was 9:30. Surely the boys would be asleep. But when Janet greeted him at the door, he could tell it had been a long night for her and was not over yet.

"They've been a bit wild tonight," she said. "Using bad words and screaming, and they won't go to sleep. They say they're waiting up for you."

"Did you turn out the lights?"

"I had to keep the night light on - otherwise they were just too upset."

"I'm sorry."

"They've been missing you. Ted keeps asking where you are, and Brian asks if it's because of the election. You know, that thing you said about running for President."

"That's nice, I guess."

"Maybe. But I should warn you - I didn't mean to, but because it's hard sometimes, I've been using you all night as the heavy. You know - 'If you don't get back into your room now, I'm telling Daddy when he gets home!'"

"Okay." This was not great news, but Porter realized that, when he had the boys alone, he was even more inclined to invoke Janet as the heavy. But he really didn't like playing the role himself, and being pre-announced for it when his absence was already exciting youthful comment could make things harder for him.

"Is that you, daddy?" The voice was Brian's, coming from the boys' room.

Porter shouted that he would be there in a minute.

He could hear the boys whispering and giggling as he took off his jacket and tie and headed to their room. At least they were in their beds, wearing their matching blue and brown Pooh pajamas, but they were sitting up and not exactly looking tired.

"Daddy," said Brian in a suspiciously sweet voice, "do you want to hear the new word that Ted learned in nursery school today?"

Janet mouthed "No" at Porter, but he decided to bite anyway. "Sure, what is it?"

Ted started shouting delightedly: "Daddy poophead! Daddy poophead!"

Brian joined in, and now they were both jumping up and down on their beds, screaming it and giggling and not listening for a good ten seconds that felt more like a minute. Then they tried to run out of the room. Standing by the door, Porter caught both of them, one in each hand, and for a second he squeezed tight to make sure they couldn't escape.

"Daddy!" Brian shouted, and Ted, "You're hurting me!"

But in a minute he had them both back in bed, Brian demanding five kisses for himself and that Ted get only three because those were their ages.

"Five for me, too!" insisted Ted.

"Five for each of you," said Porter - "Dad!", Brian started

to object - "and each of you also gets to hear a secret. I'll whisper you your secrets, but you can't tell them to each other no matter what. Is that a promise?"

Eagerly they both agreed.

The secret for Brian was: "I'm sucking away two of Ted's kisses in advance so I can give him five but you and I will know it's really three." Porter quickly made two inhaling sounds; this was how he always took extra kisses away.

The secret for Ted was, "I'm really a dinosaur." The little boy laughed and said "No you're not!"

Then they both went straight to sleep.

Porter was so exhilarated by this extraordinary triumph that for the rest of the night he knew he would be unable to bear discussing or even thinking about the office. Janet was giving him the knight-in-shining-armor look, something that he got to enjoy all too infrequently.

Why couldn't he always and everywhere handle things so smoothly? If only he could, he was thinking, he might not just be a partner by now. Maybe, as Brian had thought, he actually would be running for President.

So not until seven-thirty the next morning did he come down from the clouds and tell Janet about the scene with Stellworth the day before, and what Doberman apparently had done. They could discuss it uninterruptedly because the boys were sleeping late, evidently tired by their revels of the night before.

Janet, no Lady Macbeth but closer by a long chalk than he was to being Macbeth, could not understand his unwillingness to collaborate.

"You just don't tattle on other associates," he insisted. "There's got to be a sense of common cause, even if I'm the only one who recognizes it. Besides, what would it get me? Doberman would hate me, and he can be pretty dangerous, and even if it put him out of the picture Stellworth would get all the benefit. Don't you remember when he got me in hot water for leaving early after we had Ted?"

"We don't know for sure that it was him. Didn't he deny it?"

"Not exactly. He refused to confirm or deny it."

Janet agreed that it was his entirely his decision, one that she could not really second-guess because she did not know enough and trusted his judgment. This left Porter to wonder if maybe she was right after all. He still could not understand why Doberman would have gone so far. Even apart from the question of sane perspective, was the opportunity to do assumption of risk really so incredibly rewarding that it merited risking exposure for lying? Porter decided that he would read Doberman's section of the brief when he got the chance, although he did not mention this to Janet out of fear that she would pester him about it.

11. Between Friends

Trees die, the saying goes, so that lawyers may live. The FPHC brief filed on behalf of Barlow Industries was case in point. While merely a svelte one hundred and twenty-four pages from tip to toe, counting cover sheets, table of contents, and all, it had been duplicated enough times to merit its own little dedicated section of the national timber reserves.

There were copies for all potentially interested lawyers at Nesson & Wesson, and for that law firm's files. There were copies galore for Barlow, each FPHC commissioner, and the FPHC staff. And by mid-Thursday morning there were copies at Ashby & Cinders for all interested parties, laboriously cranked out in the A & C Xerox room from the single copy that Nesson & Wesson had seen fit to share.

In most respects, the brief had little in common with a novel by Jacqueline Susann. It entirely lacked sex, glamour, and inside dish. Still less did it naturally bring to mind the work of Stephen King. Here there was no terror, no eerie supernatural forces, no obvious source of page-turning suspense. One hardly needed the conclusion to know how it turned out, since from the very first page of argument—nay, from the very headings in the table of contents—it fairly shouted that the government's case was too weak to justify seizing assets from Barlow at this stage in the proceedings.

Still, for a few readers at least the Barlow brief brought sweaty palms and shortness of breath as they excitedly turned the pages. First Crossley and then, once the Xerox room had spit out its product, Doberman, Stellworth, and Porter, impatiently checked to see the extent to which the firm's work, and particularly for the associates their own, had been used in the final version.

Crossley, from his lofty Olympian perch, needed to keep flipping between the Ashby & Cinders version and the final one to tell how much text had survived the arduous cross-firm journey. Heads he would win, he thought complacently as he plodded through, and tails the three associates would lose. It would be nice if his leadership had sufficed on such short notice to bring Ashby & Cinders crashing into the heart of an ongoing administrative proceeding that might at some point bring billings that he could argue to the other partners were rightfully his. On the other hand, it was just too bad if three senior associates, on the verge of firm-specific death or glory, had performed so weakly that Barlow's in-house counsel would let Nesson & Wesson red-pencil their dearly-billed work into oblivion, notwithstanding the hopes for better that must have underlain the decision to consult Ashby & Cinders in the first place.

The associates' coin emphatically had two sides, however. If heads, then at least they could hope like little moons to cast their own pale reflected share of the firm's glory. Crossley could hardly slam their work in the partners' meeting next month if he planned to take credit for it. Tails was another matter, although not perhaps to be taken too much to heart. At least this was but one round in a multi-year tournament, albeit unfortunately timed if none of their work had survived. And at the partnership meeting Crossley was likely to follow his primal impulses (at least those he could indulge safely and legally) in any event.

Doberman had an additional special concern. Influence on the final product he wanted all right, but not too much of it or the wrong kind. In particular, he hoped *Tomcat Industries* had possessed the decency to bury itself forever in the murk. Even then, of course, even if it was safe from the slings and arrows of fully shepardized government counsel, one might imagine Barlow's attorneys being told, and more importantly complaining to Crossley, about the embarrassing error that had nearly been foisted upon them. One step at a time was Doberman's mantra, however; one step at a time.

To calm himself, he started by scanning the Porter and Stellworth sections. Not too much of Porter's work had survived. No surprise there; an eleventh-hour assignment to distill scientific evidence that others had been working on for some time held little promise of yielding any better—not that this would help Porter any. On jurisdiction, not too bad; Stellworth had definitely scored here and there. One could even detect what seemed to be verbatim paragraphs, and the section's conclusion if not its organization was definitely Stellworth's.

Then quickly he thumbed through assumption of risk. The harvest here was certainly as good as Stellworth's, perhaps better. But there it was near the end - the hated citation to the district court decision in *Tomcat Industries*, followed by the scarlet letters "aff'd" for affirmed, scarlet at least given what Doberman knew and the world would no doubt find out when reply briefs were filed. They were due, as it happened, at 5 o'clock on Friday, May 13, or an hour before the partnership meeting. Ordinarily, this might suggest there was no way any partner would examine it before Monday, at which point it might no longer matter to Doberman, but what if Crossley sent a messenger to get the brief promptly so he could scan it in time to attend the meeting fully armed?

Doberman began to feel slightly ill, although he tried to soothe himself by counting encouraging cliches. There's safety in numbers—how many cases did the brief cite anyway? Surely a good fifty, even exclusive of string cites. A good workman never blames his tools. He was the tool here; how incompetent could all the other attorneys be? How could they be so careless? Don't lose sight of the trees for the forest. Or rather, do lose sight of this tree. Government legal departments are often under-staffed. Perhaps they would ignore the case altogether (one could argue it was close to irrelevant since it was not a federal regulatory case), or better still fail to shepardize it themselves. If the truth still came out eventually but after the reply brief stage and therefore after the partnership meeting, then who really cared? Well, down the road Barlow, of course, and secondarily Ashby & Cinders, but that would be the extent of it.

By now it was lunchtime. He had promised to run out for a quick bite with Lyla, who had tottered back to the office, a bit early from the doctor's perspective, as soon as her fever broke. As they sat at the counter down the block with their sandwiches, she began reviewing her symptoms and speculating about when she could resume her exercise regimen and also spend the night with him.

"We'll see each other tomorrow, of course. But what about tonight, too? I probably shouldn't stay up late, and right now I think that all I could do is sleep with you—I mean, sleep next to you, not really sleep with you."

Doberman, toneless and half looking down, said "That would be great. I mean, that's too bad but it's fine." He was irritated with himself because he knew he could do so much better in responding to her appropriately. Could he of all men really find it so difficult to feign interest and enthusiasm just because Gidget was secretly the preferred flavor of the week?

Surely this single deception, standing alone, would have been no challenge, just an enjoyable flexing of the acting muscles. But this Barlow matter; really, he must be losing his touch. Right now, he would almost as soon discuss Gidget with Lyla as bring up the citation error. True, Lyla loved the office intrigue, and had vicariously shared his agonies no less than his victories. Yet this little story, at least while it remained so raw, hardly showed off the debonair, sword-flashing Zorro (no Don Diego for her) that he liked to display in his ongoing scenario of the partnership wars.

"Well, I'm sorry," Lyla broke in, really not angry though. "I guess you'll have to call Gidget if you want some real excitement."

Doberman almost gasped. Too late, he realized that this was just banter. By then Lyla, noticing his reaction, was starting to twitch like a panther. She suddenly suspected the truth, and was wondering if she could worm it out of him. A circuitous path seemed best.

"So anyway," she asked. "It's been a good week?"

He shrugged.

"You didn't seem very talkative when I called you last night."

Lyla had phoned while he was dallying on his sofa with Gidget. While Gidget had not really minded, the situation appealing to her in a half-ironic, half-masochistic way, she had contributed to the awkwardness of the situation by nibbling his ear.

Doberman explained that he had been feeling sluggish when she called. "I don't know why it is, but I've been tired all week."

"Haven't you been getting enough sleep? You certainly haven't had me to keep you up."

"No, that's the funny thing. I haven't been able to get to sleep. I've just wanted to. About all I've gotten this week is a crash course on David Letterman."

Lyla spotted an opening, and impulsively decided to go

for the kill. "That's interesting. Did you see it last night?" He nodded. "Who were his guests?"

"Just the usual. Some comedian, I think it was."

"I don't think so, Bill. I felt like staying up a bit last night, so I turned it on for a while. He had a baseball player and a rock musician."

"Whatever."

"Bill, maybe you didn't watch the Letterman show last night."

"Well, I might have dozed off a bit."

"Do you want to tell me what you really were doing last night?"

Doberman tried to look stolid.

"Maybe you were with Gidget. Think about it."

For a quarter of a second, Doberman considered trying tearful contrition. Could he argue that the nights without Lyla had been so hellishly lonely that he could not help turning somewhere, anywhere, for comfort? It seemed farfetched.

Anyway, he remembered the old saying: "Deny it. Always deny it." As in, "Who are you going to believe, honey? Me or your lying eyes?"

Yet there also was the Nixon Rule to consider. A comedian of the early 1970s, one Richard Nixon, had developed both personally and through his flacks the rich possibilities of the "nondenial denial." These were words with an escape hatch so that they meant less than they seemed to. If Nixon's wife had ever caught him in a cheap motel with another woman (not that one could imagine such a thing), he would have instructed his press secretary to say that she was being "preposterous." These were "reckless and irresponsible charges," the flack would loyally have thundered, preparatory to speculating openly about her motives.

This thinking took about another half second. Then Doberman narrowed his eyes quizzically, stared directly into

Lyla' eyes, and cocked his head to one side as if not exactly sure
what he was hearing.

"Me and Gidget O'Malley?!?" (This was no time for proper
grammar.) "That's ridiculous. What would I be doing with
her?"

"You tell me."

"It's absurd. You must still have a fever. I have half a mind
to walk out of here."

Lyla could see the game slipping away. "Well, I don't know.
I just thought—you looked like you were thinking—and you
know you like her."

"I know you like to think so."

"I don't know. Let's forget about it. Maybe I'm wrong."

"Maybe you are wrong, and maybe you should have
thought about that possibility before you made this - this
laughable accusation."

"Well, in that case I'm sorry."

Doberman pouted.

"I'm sorry, Bill. What do you want from me? I apologize.
I'm sorry."

In truth, Lyla was not fully placated. While knowing that
she had blown it for now and moderately impressed by his
reaction, she felt that careful observation over a number of days
would be necessary before he could be fully exonerated.

Still, Doberman felt revived now that the gauntlet, or one
of them anyway, was down. The next few hours passed quickly,
albeit only livened by a furtive phone call to warn Gidget that
they would have to be very cautious for a while.

At seven, he was due home to host Lyla, who still wanted
a quiet evening with him, perhaps now more than ever. Just
before leaving, he rushed off to find Cinders, with no real plan
in mind beyond watering the seeds already planted. Looking
for Cinders at this hour was a bit of a long shot, although well
worth it since the competition from phone calls would be
reduced. He knew that the old boy generally did not stay late

in the office once the week had begun wearing on. He had not guessed, however, that the old boy would entertain the same suspicion about him.

"William, I'm glad you're still here," said an unusually genial Cinders. "I tried to call you a moment ago. I was just wondering if you had left early."

"Early?" Doberman replied, attempting a light laugh. "Why, it's not even six-thirty. In my book, nothing before seven is even late enough to be early."

Cinders looked at him blankly, unable to follow this.

"I mean, I'm happy if I can get out of here by seven. Not happy, I mean, because I enjoy working here, but contented. Well, not contented, exactly, because I'm sure there's always more to think about, but—but at least I don't feel like I'm cheating anyone. Not - not that I ever do."

"Good. And you knew that I wanted to see you."

"I certainly hoped so. There's something I wanted to talk about."

"So you got my message just now?"

"I didn't get a message. Nobody tells me anything."

"Very well, then. I wanted to see you." Cinders hemmed dramatically, and Doberman leaned forward in his seat.

"I have a sudden problem. I need a rifleshot."

Some—say, his fallen rivals from the old days—might have argued that a rifleshot was exactly what Cinders needed. He meant the term, however, in a strictly metaphorical sense. A "rifleshot," in law firm lingo, is an assignment to research an extremely narrow legal issue that needs to be resolved as fast as possible, by finding, for example, a case precisely on point or the details of an obscure statute.

"I have a meeting at ten tomorrow morning," Cinders continued. "By that time, I need the answer to several questions about New Jersey law concerning reversionary trusts. I imagine it would take no more than an hour of research. You can just put the key points in a memo, and leave it on my desk."

Doberman grabbed the explanatory paperwork and expressed his keen delight. He knew, however, that partners, when giving out assignments, discount research time by fifty to seventy-five percent. Two to four hours, then, was the likely requirement. Lyla would not be very pleased just now when he called to cancel on her.

"Very good," Cinders said to him. "And I'm glad to hear that I'm not keeping you here late."

"Not at all."

"By the way, do you know where I'm having lunch tomorrow? Friends of the Opera. Stop by and see me in the afternoon. I'll tell you how it went, and you can fill me in then if I need any follow-up on reversionary trusts."

"About two o'clock?"

"Say 2:15 to be safe. Leave a note for my secretary as you go, so she'll put it on my calendar."

For a second, Doberman could almost imagine that Cinders, when mentioning the lunch, had been on the verge of nudging him playfully in the ribs. This was bliss undreamt of. Where was Cinders going when he left the office? Maybe to the Harvard Club for a drink; to alums his age it seemed to be a hot spot. Perhaps, in the course of the libations, some fellow old fogy would nudge him in the ribs and say, "Cedric, old fellow, you're one of a kind," and he'd reply: "I used to think so, but I've got this young associate, he reminds me of me . . . " The fantasy left Doberman blushing.

To call Lyla's answering machine at home, then the doorman of his building in case she was already headed there, was the work of an instant. It was just as well not to talk to her now. He was just congratulating himself on his good fortune and gearing up for reversionary trusts when he heard a timid knock on his door. He barked permission to enter, and saw Porter lingering indecisively at the threshold before lurching forward, almost tripping in the process, to take a seat.

"Bill, there's something I have to talk to you about." He

was nervous this time, not just awkward and bashful as usual. "I think there's a mistake in your section of the Barlow brief. You're probably not aware of it."

Porter had read the Barlow brief, and noticed a citation to a case called *Tomcat Industries* at which he had raised an eyebrow. It seemed familiar from the Commercial Law Updates that were placed each morning in every lawyer's In box. He remembered its being reversed on rehearing, an unusual turn of events although the case had been of no special interest at the time. He had checked the Ashby & Cinders brief, and there it was too, word for word the same. This had to be Doberman's error, but presumably everyone else had missed it too.

"Oh, I know about it," Doberman said wearily. Was he to have no peace? Must everything be a struggle? He knew he could square Porter if he really put his mind to it, but it seemed so unfair that he should have to do it right now. Business, however, was definitely business.

So Doberman began by noting that it was no longer Ashby & Cinders' error. The other guys had filed the final brief, and they were now responsible.

Also, to confess error now would help no one. Ashby & Cinders was trying to land this client. The court would get it right soon enough. And anyway the big partnership meeting was coming up. Was that the real point? Doberman had thought that he and Porter—here a daring glance to see if he could get away with this—were friends. Colleagues had to stick together.

Porter burbled something about a higher loyalty.

Now a sneer was in order, and duly it was provided. All this talk of loyalty was very nice, but obviously Porter's real motivation was to stab a rival in the back. And then, presumably, to kick him when he was down. Maybe after that, to start stomping on him.

Porter blushed. He was not like this. Other people might be, but not him. Doberman pressed the attack, and after several minutes Porter surrendered, his sense of legal rectitude proving weaker than his aversion to helping himself. He staggered to the door, looking as browbeaten as he always looked beetle-browed, and withdrew.

Three hours of research and one chilly phone message from Lyla later, Doberman found himself craving a stiff drink. On the way home, however, he came up with a better idea. He wanted to see Gidget again, but Washington was not safe at this time. So why not a weekend in New York? Perhaps the following weekend, since the one coming right up was too soon for all the necessary arrangements.

This would be business, however, as well as pleasure. The Lyla-Gidget situation was unstable, and he could not tolerate that with everything else that was going on. Gidget might well be temporary, but for now was quite important. Lyla was important in the long haul, keeping in mind her father at Carp, Stone, & Tyler as a fallback position, but for the moment she was too vexing and impatient. It was time at last to implement a scheme that he had dreamed up long ago, merely as an imagined or fantasy exercise in debonair derring-do, never at the time imagining that he would actually try it some day. It was time, in short, for the Alpha Plan, also known as Project Victory.

_12._ Project Victory

The glory that was Rome – Disneyland – the Apollo space program – none of these was built in a day. The same would hold for Project Victory, although here a week would suffice. Essentially a tricky billiards shot, it demanded that the balls be aligned just so. Then strike the cue ball just so, and more importantly than anything the next shot would be aligned just so.

Thursday night had found Doberman in a state of high excitement and irritation, unfortunately giving him his fourth straight (albeit first Gidget-free) night of little sleep. How could he not be excited, with the prospect looming before him of a cozy tete-a-tete with Cinders on matters great and small? Or make that, on prospective new clients mid-sized and rifleshots small. Yet how to help being irritated by all the rest? Porter must stay squelched, and preliminary arrangements be painstakingly made for what he hoped would be the ultimate glory of Project Victory.

Friday morning seeped forward like motor oil from a loose gasket. There were documents to proof, and research for a client memo that the billing partner would be red-penciling extensively no matter what he did. Nothing to really sink one's teeth into. The only challenge was being certain to avoid even the slightest whisper of an actual or arguable error so late in the proceedings.

Also, Lyla was expecting him for Friday night through Sunday. He could request time off for work on Saturday and Sunday as needed, but otherwise few motions were likely to be granted. His corpus must be habeased, and that was that.

While Lyla was out at lunch, he placed a furtive phone call to Gidget.

"So, how was your Thursday night?" she asked, having known that he planned to spend it with Lyla.

Doberman explained that he had spent it instead with New Jersey reversionary trusts. "But I'll be spending the whole weekend with her. She's suspicious. We're going to have to be very careful."

"Poor Bill. If one of his girlfriends isn't bothering him, it's the other."

"Gidget, I hope you understand the situation. I'd really like to see you again, but right now things are dicey."

"Is any of it up to you?"

"Not really. She must have smelled you on me. She caught on immediately. I denied it, but I know she's thinking: of course he denied it."

Gidget was philosophical. She did not want to hurt Lyla's feelings. But in her tautological viewpoint, the affair with Doberman had happened. Ergo, it had been meant to happen. Ergo, whatever was going to happen would happen. Everything would take care of itself, one way or another. She could not really believe that she would lose him any time soon, but the bare prospect of it created a delicious uncertainty, postponing any ambivalence about a more favorable outcome.

Having gotten to this point, Doberman decided that it was time for the carrot. Time, moreover, to place the first ball in its spot on the billiard table.

"Are you doing anything next weekend?" he asked quickly, aiming for the impression of a blurt.

"Maybe. Should I try to keep it open?"

"How would you like to spend it with me in New York?"

"Is that really safe? She could have spies there, you know."

"You're joking."

"Maybe I'm afraid that you're joking."

"I'm not. This is definite. A total promise. No cancellation possible." You could never really say this as an Ashby & Cinders associate, but Doberman was willing to gamble.

Gidget agreed. She was starting to find this positively romantic. She had not had to conceal a love affair since sleeping with her boyfriend in junior high school, an act that she hid from her parents since they took the position, unusually conservative for southern California, that girls should not go all the way before age fifteen.

The day's turn to excitement was only starting, however. At 2:12, Doberman completed and marked off another tenth of a billable hour on his timesheet and headed to Cinders' office. Between the great man's phone calls, he ascertained that the trust memo was fine. Nothing further need be done with it. The Friends of the Opera lunch, however, had been postponed for a week. Here Cinders turned expansive.

"I should really take you sometime, or maybe Stellworth if you're busy. It's a nice group. The Opera's main purpose is fund-raising, but they know you need to listen to people first, hear their opinions. We talk about recent performances, possible future ones, the performers we might like to see ... Do you want to hear something amusing?"

"What?"

"I am probably the poorest man there. Also from the humblest background ... Also the only one there apart from the opera company who hopes to make money from the lunch

… Remind me again about *Der Meistersinger*. Traversi was good, you said, and Luga bad?"

"Not so much 'bad,' I'd say, as disappointing. After the build-up, you know. She's a voice, yes, but not much else."

Cinders emitted a low sound, apparently a kind of chuckle. "Good, good. I should almost give you a quarter-point if I land the client."

Fat chance, of course. A hungry Allosaurus would sooner have shared a fresh kill than Cinders the financial reward from rainmaking (the term of art for drumming up new business). Still, the thought was nice enough to help make the rest of the day more bearable. This is boring, Doberman's right brain would say as he nailed down a research point or proofed a memo. Yes, but Cinders is starting to associate me with rainmaking, his left brain would answer. The Pavlovian implications were too obvious to need underlining even in braintalk.

By the time he left for home to meet Lyla, fatigue was starting to replace elation, but this wasn't all bad. Perhaps he could milk it for the right intermediate level of verisimilitude. I'm tired because I didn't sleep last night, he'd say. I'm just so worried about … Uncle Wilmer? No, better to use Uncle Charlie. Lyla had met Charlie once.

They were sitting at dinner in a restaurant near his apartment, the conversation lagging from things best left unsaid, when Lyla observed that he looked tired.

"I know I do. Or at least I'm not surprised. I didn't sleep much last night. Even when I finished the trust memo, I was just so worried about my Uncle Charlie."

It came out sounding a little too glib, a bit too smooth, just as it was supposed to.

"What about him?"

Doberman shrugged.

"Is he the one from Pennsylvania?" she asked.

"Yes. Specifically Wilkes-Barre. My father's brother." This, to help her be sure of the last name. "He called me last night. He's had, well, a stroke."

"Oh, that's too bad! But if he's already making phone calls I guess it can't be too bad."

"Well, it's not too good either. Just a minor stroke, but now he's not walking well, and they're afraid of a follow-up stroke. He's in the hospital for observation. He should be out in a few days. He wants me to visit him. Maybe next weekend."

"Is there anything you can really do for him? I didn't think you were that close."

"Well, he asked me. I don't really know why. Maybe I should go."

"Should I come too?"

Doberman pursed his lips thoughtfully. "That's an idea. No, I think not. If he's in a bathrobe or something, not looking or feeling his best …"

Lyla was perplexed. Surely he wouldn't make this up, but she knew from experience that he liked to avoid her during periods of high suspicion, even if he was innocent. "I didn't think he was so important to you. Does it just sound better to you than spending the weekend with me?"

"Not at all. You know there's nothing I'd like as much as to spend next weekend with you." This was literally true. There was nothing he would like exactly as much, neither more nor less.

There was a pause, and Doberman shrugged again. "Why don't we say I won't go after all. Unless he has another stroke or a scare or something."

The night was disappointing as reunions go, Doberman being as tired as his affect had suggested. The next night was a little better, but still he seemed unusually distant. He didn't even want to discuss the latest office politics. He did make a comment, with surprising emphasis it seemed, to the effect that he was close to earning 20,000 United frequent flyer miles.

"I'm definitely taking them wherever I go, unless they don't go there. Even if it's New York and I could take the shuttle."

But he hadn't looked into whether United flew to Wilkes Barre or points nearby.

The ensuing week brought further odd developments. Doberman worked late every night, even though nothing unusual was afoot, citing only the approaching partnership decision and the possibility that he would need to keep the weekend open for Uncle Charlie. Gidget, Lyla heard through the office grapevine, had told several people that she was going to New York for the weekend. The details and broader circumstances were unknown. For a while Uncle Charlie seemed better, but then on Thursday he had a follow-up stroke, just a very little one really, you almost might call it just a tremor, but still Doberman now felt that he should definitely go.

So Lyla was uneasy as they said goodbye in his office on Friday afternoon.

"Should I call you? Where are you staying?" she asked.

"I don't have it with me. Why don't I call you when I can?"

Could appearances be deceiving? They rarely are, of course, even when they appear to be. But this time the trail of clues seemed almost too obvious. Surely Doberman was defter than this, and hence deserved the Nixon Watergate defense: "He can't be guilty. Even if he's slimy enough, he's not that stupid."

Had Lyla observed the 8 o'clock Washington to New York shuttle, however, she would have concluded, like Barry Goldwater before her, that yes, apparently Nixon is that stupid. Doberman and Gidget were unmistakably snuggling in Row 7. Having not seen each other for nine whole days except once briefly in the hallway, and having even kept their phone conversations to a prudent minimum, they were very happy to be together again, and in entirely safe circumstances.

"You told people you were going to New York?" he asked.

"Yes, just like you said I should. What was that all about? But I didn't breathe a whisper about your coming with me."

"Great. I have almost the whole weekend free. No commitments except for one short meeting that I have to go to on Sunday morning. It won't take more than an hour."

On the plane they both had a drink, and when they arrived at their Midtown hotel they had another one. They did not go out again, choosing instead to have a late dinner sent up to their room.

This had been Gidget's suggestion, but Doberman moved swiftly to make the agenda his own. He held back as they ordered dinner, surprising her by agreeing that she should order a cheeseburger, and to her still greater surprise ordering one himself.

"You can't really do any better than that on room service anyway," he said. "And anyway, I have nothing against cheeseburgers."

He did, however, insist on their taking splits of champagne rather than a bottle of red wine from the room's minibar. Gidget was concerned that the champagne would give her a headache, but Doberman explained that this only happened with the cheaper brands.

"I guess I'll just have to trust you on this one." Gidget smiled at him and gravely shook her head. "Champagne and cheeseburgers. Bill, you're really spoiling me. I'm not sure how anything else I ever do will stand up to this."

After dinner he put the plates outside the door, paused in the coat closet to paw at his luggage, and emerged clutching three items wrapped in newspaper. They turned out to be scented dark blue candles that were set in wide glass bases. Ceremoniously he lit them, placing one on each of the nightstands on the sides of the bed and one on the dresser across. Then with a flourish he turned out all the lights.

Doberman sat down on the side of the bed and took off his shoes and socks. Gidget had already removed hers upon entering the room.

"Come over here," he said. She came right over and sat next to him, each with an arm around the other. They turned to face each other and started to kiss, lips smooshed together and tongues softly probing.

He unbuttoned her top and slipped it off as she cooperated by raising her arms. Then, after stroking her shoulders, arms, and stomach in turn, he slid his hands up to cup her breasts. After a moment he unsnapped her bra.

"I'm glad the snap is in the front," he said.

Gidget had her eyes closed and wasn't saying anything.

"I love your nipples. I was so surprised that they're brown. I was thinking they'd be pink like most of the time they are."

She moved her face back an inch to speak but kept her eyes closed. "You thought you had it all worked out? Visualized me from tip to toe before you saw anything?"

"Pretty much."

"Anything else to report on? Moles or freckles, maybe?"

"Everything was great. 11 on a scale of 10."

"Such a smooth talker."

He reached under her skirt and she gave a sigh and pressed back against him. For some minutes they were silent except for their breathing.

At length, as they lay together on the bed, she nude and he still fully dressed, she reached over to unbutton his shirt. He put up his hand to grab the back of hers and stop her.

Surprised, she looked into his eyes. "I thought you like it when I take off your clothes."

"I do. Very much. But this time, to be different, I'm going to stay dressed."

Seeing her brow furrow, he quickly added: "I didn't say zipped, just dressed."

He took off his belt so it wouldn't press on her. In due course he unbuttoned and unzipped his pants and then for fifteen minutes, or maybe it was even twenty, they made love in the missionary position without a condom.

After another couple of minutes he slid off to the side but continued holding her.

"That was interesting," she said. "I actually liked it and I didn't think I would."

"I should have told you up front; I think of this as going both ways. So why don't you get dressed in a couple of minutes and then you can undress me."

"Okay... I don't have a front zipper, you know."

"That's okay. You can pull things down a bit if you have to. And you can be on top this time."

"Okay."

Their lovemaking took a couple of minutes less this time because he got more excited even though they had just done it so recently.

"How did you get the idea of doing it like this?" she asked as they lay together again, at last both naked after she had removed her clothes.

"Oh, I just thought it would be interesting. It's actually a first for me. I mean, doing it exactly this way ... I think the power thing is what makes it interesting. You know, one person is dressed and the other isn't."

"You and power."

"Well, we did do it both ways."

"That's true."

"From now on, a rule," Doberman said. "I promise. No clothes for either of us unless we're going out or something."

"Or calling room service."

"Or we want to be dressed. Or whatever."

They slept in for a late room service breakfast on Saturday

morning, donning terry-cloth bathrobes from the coat closet when it came. Then they took a cozy shower together and put on fresh outfits, since Doberman was insisting that they go out. Gidget had never been to New York before, and he was eager to show her some of the principal attractions. She agreed on condition that they stay out of the subway, which she had heard was dirty and dangerous. It could give her claustrophobia, even though the Washington Metro was fine.

They walked through a sector of Central Park that he promised would be safe, then cabbed down to Battery Park to see the Statue of Liberty before taking the Circle Line cruise around Manhattan, these being activities that she had chosen over museum visits. Late in the afternoon they went to the World Trade Center, which she had always wanted to see, but the glassed-in roof deck gave her vertigo. So they headed back to the hotel, and it was all he could do later to talk her out of room service again. Finally she agreed to take a cab to Chinatown, but she didn't like the small streets or the smells, and asked for a restaurant that she thought had slightly better atmosphere than the rest, but that he thought looked touristy. Once there, she vetoed his more venturesome menu suggestions. At least he was able to talk her out of the chicken chow mein.

Dessert in Little Italy was better, and a restored Gidget agreed to take the subway from Canal Street back to midtown. They were probably no more than a hundred feet from the station where they would be exiting when the train stopped abruptly and, for about thirty seconds, the lights went out. Even after they came back on, the train did not move for another fifteen minutes. Gidget began closing her eyes and whispering that she had to get out of there.

She continued to feel skittish when they emerged, and asked Doberman not to walk too close or to put his arm around her. Back in the hotel, the first elevator was too crowded for her, so they had to wait for the second. Back in their room, for the first time since the first time, he had to work at coaxing her into bed with him.

By the time they were lying together afterwards, she had recovered sufficiently to stroke his chin while mock-complaining about mistreatment.

"First you can't see me for days and days. Then you drag me to a strange town, full of crazy people, and finally you trap me in a dirty underground dungeon."

"Imagine what I'll do if you don't behave."

She replied by biting his finger.

"Do you think of me as a big bad wolf?" he asked hopefully.

"No, you're more of a big sweetie"—a view that already was by no means universal, and on the verge in some quarters of becoming even less so.

On Sunday, Doberman called Lyla when he knew she was in the health club, and left a message promising to call again within the hour if he could (he knew he wouldn't). She shouldn't bother to call him; it wasn't necessary, and anyway he had left no return number. Then he kissed Gidget and left for his appointment. He returned to the hotel room within the promised time, looking smug but offering no explanation.

Lyla, meanwhile, had been wrestling with her suspicions all weekend. She might as well have been pulling petals off a daisy, intoning "He's a slimeball—he's not. He's a slimeball…" Or better—why mince words about the man she nonetheless loved?—"He's *my* slimeball—he's not. He's *my* slimeball—he's not…"

She had kept Doris in the dark, apart from mentioning that Bill would be away for the weekend because his uncle was sick. What Mom would say if more fully informed was all too obvious, and also all too painful because it was half, but only half, of what Lyla was saying to herself. But the timing of his phone call (she knew he knew her schedule), along with his failure to leave his number or subsequently call back, were the final straws.

"Mom," she finally said over the salad they were sharing as an early dinner, "I'm getting a bit anxious. It's about Bill."

"I figured. What did he say in his message?"

"Nothing. But he deliberately called when I was out. And I can't reach him, and he's not calling back, and also there are some other reasons why I think he's up to something."

Mother heard Lyla out and was surprisingly measured. Don't convict him of anything right off the bat, she suggested. Just find out for yourself what's really going on, even if it takes some initiative. But meanwhile don't torture yourself. There's plenty of time later to decide what to do, if it turns out that there's a problem. She retreated into her room to watch television and give Lyla some privacy.

Lyla, taking deep breaths to calm herself, called Wilkes Barre information and got the phone numbers for the city's three main hospitals. None had any record of admitting a Charles Doberman in the last two weeks. Then she called information again for Uncle Charlie's home number, and promptly got him on the line.

"Stroke? Me? Is this supposed to be funny? I don't think it is," he said before hanging up on her.

New York it had to be then, with Gidget. She could add two and two as well as the next person. Could she catch the guilty couple in flagrante, at least in the sense of walking off the plane together? What flight would they take? The shuttle would be a wild goose chase, there being two of them that arrived at alternating half hours. Then again, he had said something about United Airlines, although perhaps this was disinformation too. She decided to try her luck with United Airlines flight information.

The first United switchboard operator who Lyla reached would not move off the point that the names of people who make reservations are confidential. The second said the computers were down. The third did not care if Lyla was, as she insisted, the sister of a passenger whose father was deathly ill. Upon hearing Lyla's real reason for wanting the information, however, she relented, and told her that William Doberman was expected at National Airport at 9:03 p.m. on Flight 357. He was traveling by himself. No one named O'Malley, or even Mrs. Doberman, was booked on the flight.

In New York, meanwhile, Doberman sent Gidget home first by the shuttle, and arrived alone at LaGuardia in plenty of time for Flight 357. Back in Washington, Lyla missed him coming off the airplane, although he lingered helpfully for a moment or two by the gate, but she caught up with him in the luggage area. He feigned delighted shock, mingled with embarrassment, at seeing her there.

"So how's your uncle?" she asked, only her pallor and shortness of breath betraying her emotion. She resisted an attempted embrace, her eyes roving about to see if Gidget was anywhere in the area.

"He's actually fine. It seems to have been a false alarm."

"And how was Wilkes Barre?"

"Wilkes Barre is Wilkes Barre."

"Did you enjoy yourself?"

"Not especially."

"Do you think you'll be returning soon?"

"Probably not."

"I see." Lyla's color was starting to heighten. "Bill," she said slowly, "let me tell you something." She paused to swallow. "Bill, you're a liar."

"Huh? Me? A liar, you say?"

"You weren't in Wilkes Barre this weekend."

"I wasn't?"

"And you didn't see your uncle. You may have seen a lot of someone who you and I both know, but it wasn't your uncle."

Doberman nodded. "I can see your point. After all, I am

picking up my luggage by the sign for the flight from New York."

Lyla, startled by this change of tactics, was silent.

"You probably want to know why I went to New York and, well, if you insist, lied about it," he said sympathetically, like an adult explaining something to a child.

"That's right."

"In that case, you'll be happy to know that I can explain everything."

"Let's hear it. This had better be good."

"You want to hear it now?" he asked, as if this were a disconcerting surprise.

"Sure. You're clever enough to think of something."

"I have a better idea. Why don't you just trust me?"

Lyla was too stunned even to reply. He must really be losing his touch.

"Trust is important, Lyla," he admonished, wagging his finger. "You can't have a relationship without it."

"I'll say." Lyla took a deep breath. "You're a swine," she said. "Do you really think I'm that stupid? Do you think you can just run off to New York with Gidget and lie to me about it, and I'll never suspect a thing? I know all about you guys. I bet you've just spent the whole weekend fucking in a hotel room."

Doberman was struck by her perceptiveness. How well she understood Gidget's preferred method of visiting the greatest city in the world. Rather than let this show, however, he took two steps back, and gestured dramatically, one hand splayed outward in the manner of an orator and the other striking his chest.

"You know, Lyla, I've had just about enough of this." He spoke with none of his usual buoyancy, employing instead a quiet, clipped, ominous tone. "I think I've had enough of your paranoia and insane jealousy. I know I've had enough of your insecurity."

Lyla gulped, and Doberman gestured again.

"I guess I was stupid," he said. "I thought that maybe if I gave you more certainty it would make a difference. And that's why I went to New York this weekend."

He reached with one hand into his pocket. "At this point, though, I don't think I even want to bother. Just forget about it. Maybe I'll even give Gidget a call when I get home. She must be worth my time if she's half as exciting as you seem to think she is.

"Just for the record, though, there's something I want to show you. I was planning to wait a week or two until the proper moment, but now it doesn't matter. Here, this is why I went to New York this weekend. You know the diamond district there? I have a connection. This was going to be for you," he said.

He pulled out of his pocket a familiar type of little black box. Opening it deftly with two fingers, he showed her a diamond engagement ring sitting inside. Then he snapped it shut, put it back in his pocket, turned on his heel, and left her standing there, his exit in the very best stage tradition.

Only when Doberman had disappeared from her sight did he permit himself to pump a fist in triumph. His plan had worked perfectly. So what about the cash out of pocket for the ring, he thought. Maybe Lyla would end up getting it anyway, at least if he didn't make partner. But for now he was free and she was properly chastened. In the short run, he could do what he liked. Eventually he might forgive her, but not until he was good and ready. In any event, diamonds are supposed to be such a good investment.

Meanwhile Lyla, numb and with her fingers tingling as if someone had slammed her in the funnybone, stumbled to the DC National Metro stop that would be taking her home. Probably it was fortunate that DC National was at the end of the line, since otherwise she might have had a fifty percent chance of boarding the train in the wrong direction.

She couldn't believe what had just happened, yet it had to be true.

I'm not going to talk about it, I'm not going to talk about it, she kept saying to herself, knowing that Mother would be waiting up to hear what had happened.

When Lyla got home, she said: "We broke up but I don't want to talk about it," before she had even taken her key out of the lock.

"I'm sorry," Mom said, which was nice as a gesture, but Lyla couldn't help snapping back, "I just don't want to talk about it." She took off her jacket, placed it carefully on a hanger in the closet, smoothed it with her fingers, walked deliberately to her room, and closed the door, pushing it firmly to make sure that it would stay shut.

13. The Other Shoe Drops

When tabloid writers need a human interest story to fill up the back pages, the possible angles may include sledgehammer irony. As in: "On Friday, April 15, Canton Paxler won $10 million in the lottery. Ironically, only minutes before the drawing, he had fallen from the ninety-fourth floor of an office building."

Doberman, had he known more, might have identified with Canton Paxler as he headed home from the airport, flushed with the success of Project Victory. A six-mile comet, or rather two of them, were heading for his little Cretaceous paradise, threatening, if they hit like the real one sixty-five million years ago, to set off firestorms followed by the threat of nuclear winter.

Gravitational perturbations emanating from Porter were the perhaps unlikely source of the first threatened strike from the heavens. Porter had been wrestling with his thoughts about the citation error that Doberman was insisting should go uncorrected. Officers of the court, or equally of an administrative agency, are not supposed to mislead, at least not beyond accepted bounds. Fudge or misinterpret a case, yes, but keep an inaccurate citation in place, surely not. Ashby & Cinders was officially of counsel, which made it an officially involved party. Plus, it seemed unlikely that the firm could avoid its share of the blame for a citation error that came from its own memo, and that seemed certain to be detected at the reply brief stage of the proceedings.

Indeed, the reply brief stage might be a double whammy. Barlow had decided that Nesson & Wesson should draft the reply brief and Ashby & Cinders then review it. While this was in some respects a plum position - freedom to criticize without responsibility - it meant that the error might first be conceded in the draft (perhaps with a pencilled note in the client's copy blaming it on Ashby & Cinders), and then get a full body slam in the government reply brief. This would certainly be bad news for the firm's broader relationship with Barlow.

The problem was that Porter couldn't really ask anyone at the office what to do without actually resolving the problem through disclosure. Just asking would be like stopping by Secret Service headquarters to inquire, "Should I report it to you—would you take an interest—if someone I know is making death threats against the President?"

Janet, however, he could and indeed must talk to, although he wanted an occasion when they were not too tired and could really focus (meaning that there must be not be any boys in the vicinity.) His chance came on a rare Saturday night out, made possible by Janet's discovery of a new babysitter, the college student daughter of an older couple from down the block. Thus, right around the time when Doberman and Gidget were wandering hand in hand through Chinatown together. Porter and Janet were seated at a restaurant in Washington's own two-block Chinatown, picking away at a whole steamed fish. She was using her chopsticks deftly enough, but he had given up and switched to a fork after almost landing a prawn on her lap during the appetizer course. He had not yet worked the conversation around to Doberman's citation error and boldfaced response to disclosure of same, but was thinking he might do so soon.

Dinner talk on the Porters' nights out followed a consistent pattern. Long gone were the meandering exchanges of ideas from when they first met - say, concerning a class that one of them was taking, or the books they were reading, or perhaps a Bergman or Truffaut film they had seen together on campus the other night. They no longer were taking classes, or for that matter reading books or seeing movies. So instead what usually happened was that they would discuss Brian and Ted for a while, generally with Janet in the lead, and then at some point switch to Ashby & Cinders with Arnold in the lead for a discussion of his work pressures. Both topics could be absorbing enough, especially to the discussion leader, but the overall effect was less relaxing than either of them might have liked. They sometimes made resolutions to try avoiding both topics, but this was hard for them to do even in their own interior monologues.

Naturally enough, then, they began on this night by picking apart the babysitter for a while - perhaps a kind of rehearsal for the steamed fish. The girl had seemed nice enough to Janet in a short interview, but would she really engage with the boys? How patient was she? Would she give them too much dessert, or drug them with television so she could do her classwork or talk on the phone? Did she have a boyfriend, and might he come over without authorization?

Next came Brian's and Ted's current state of interaction and development. Porter decided to nudge this in the more broadly ruminative direction of their conversations of times past.

"You know, it's occurred to me," he said, "remember how people in the 1960s used to talk about living totally in the moment? Forget the future, forget the past, it's just about now, all that stuff?"

Janet nodded. Two years older than him, she had heard

it all at the time, though never finding it quite as interesting as he had.

"That's exactly what Brian and Ted do," he continued. "Just their age makes them, in effect, these incredible 1960s people. One moment they're hungry, and if you don't bring them a Pop Tart immediately, they're in agony. The next moment they don't even want it any more. Or they're fighting and 'Ted's not my friend,' but the next moment it's 'Look, Ted, isn't this cool,' and then the moment after that it's, I don't know, they want to eat again or something."

"They're kids."

"I know. But my point is that back then, no one thought of that spontaneous, in-the-moment stuff as being just like little kids, which is exactly what it is. The funny thing is how unappealing it seems, once you really get to see it in action. Unappealing to really be that way, I mean. It's like lambs to the slaughter."

"Do you think Brian and Ted are unhappy?"

"No, not at all. They're doing great. It's just that seeing them brings it home to me in a way, how much I'd hate to really be like that, at least now. It's like they have no control over anything."

Janet gave him a raised-eyebrows look, and he responded with a short laugh.

"I know," he said. "Whereas I have so much control over everything in my life."

"You've been seeming distracted lately," Janet said. Evidently she was ready to drop the kids, maybe figuring from this riff that he was tiring of the subject. "Is it just because of the partners' meeting coming up?"

"That's probably most of it."

"And you're still expecting to get screwed."

"Pretty much."

"Even though they've kept you all these years."

"Well, all that means is they think my work is good

enough. Otherwise, they would have kicked me out inside of six months. They're making good money off me now. But they're not going to split their profits with me, and invite me forever to all their partner lunches, just because I do good legal research. Heck, they'd be stupid to reward me just for that, when it isn't even what I'd be doing most of the time as a partner."

"Haven't they ever heard of the Peter principle? Or maybe I should say, haven't they ever not heard of it?"

"Thanks a lot. I probably could learn to do the other stuff reasonably well, at least other than hustling new clients. And a lot of them don't do that well anyway. But it's mainly a social contest at this point, and I'm just not good at that stuff."

"You should just try to hold your head up a bit more. Make yourself play the game. Look at how great you are with the boys sometimes."

"Sometimes ... But the thing about the office is, it's like high school. I used to freeze up there, too."

Porter paused to pick a bone out of his teeth, and waved to the hovering waiters to take away the fish. Now was really the time to mention Doberman's citation error, but still he shied away from the subject. What if she insisted that telling Crossley would be the smart thing and also the right thing to do, and he couldn't disagree with her but still didn't really want to do it?

Meanwhile, the fortune cookies arrived. Janet opened hers first and read it: "Early to rise late to bed makes man wise and wealthy but dead." She handed it to him.

"I guess they save money on the punctuation," he said.

"You should have gotten that one."

"Oh, come on. I'm not that bad as that. I get some sleep every now and then."

"You do go to bed sometimes." She was generally pretty nice about his being so restless when he couldn't sleep.

"They must have special fortune cookies for lawyers," he said.

"I'm not a lawyer."

"Well, make that for lawyers and their ilk. By now you're honorary ilk."

"Thanks. But what does yours say?"

He cracked his cookie open, shoved half of it into his mouth, and read the little slip of paper out loud before swallowing:

"'The peacock gets killed for its plumage.' This is great. Maybe all the fortune cookies are morbid here. But actually I like this one. In context it's almost hopeful. I'm definitely not the office peacock."

Indeed, among the associates that would have to be Doberman. With an omen like this, Porter could wait no longer, and briskly he gave Janet the facts in re. *Tomcat Industries.*

"He was just so unapologetic. It was amazing. He made me out to be the bad guy if I tried to clear things up."

"And you accepted that."

"Well, in effect I guess I have so far."

Janet thought that, as dilemmas go, this one was pretty darned simple. Just go right ahead and tell Crossley. Certainly the most you could have owed Doberman is a warning in advance, and you've already given him that. Telling Crossley is the right thing to do, and it might even be in your interest.

Principles plus interest, Porter was thinking. It's beginning to sound like a loan.

Nonetheless, he remained reluctant. He just didn't want to feel blood on his hands. Whether Doberman got angry with him or not was not quite the point, although certainly another confrontation would be no fun. Just what was the point was hard to articulate. So Porter promised only that he would make a decision in the next day or two, and let Janet know about it.

By Sunday morning, he realized with greater clarity that he was simply feeling squeamish. Still, he felt inclined to indulge this feeling as best he could. Let Doberman suffer, let Porter even be the detectable if indirect cause of the suffering, but let someone else be responsible for the close-in dirty work.

The one and only obvious dirty worker at hand was Stellworth. So Porter, after spending most of Sunday at home, cornered the aging former choirboy in the library at about 6 o'clock, right while Doberman was clapping Gidget into a shuttle-bound taxicab. All at once Porter spilled the goods in a whisper, under terms of strict confidence that both he and Stellworth realized were not worth the paper they weren't printed on.

Stellworth, as the saying goes, was shocked and stunned. Once he grasped the essential facts and had confirmed in Shepard's the reversal of *Tomcat Industries*, he waived Porter away without even a reproach for sitting on the secret for so long.

Staggering slowly back to his office, Stellworth told himself: here it is at last, triumph total and absolute. There was no way out for Doberman. This blunder, publicized properly, would doom his career.

With a keen sense of melodrama, Stellworth reached into the bookshelves behind his desk and pulled out the binder containing the Ashby & Cinders directory. Turning to Doberman's page, he tore it out, crumpled it, and threw it in the trash. As Stalin might have said, although Stellworth was not accustomed to quoting Communists, Doberman was about to be relegated to the dustbin of history.

Stellworth could imagine a number of possible scenarios for Doberman's reaction. In one, he would fall to the floor, grab Stellworth's knees, and blubber incoherent prayers for mercy. This would be highly distasteful. In another, Doberman would sink to his own knees and grovel from there. This would be no better. Stellworth tut-tutted haughtily. It was simply disgraceful how little pride and dignity Doberman showed in all these scenarios.

He's probably expecting a garden party on partnership day, Stellworth thought. But me, I'll make that garden party look like a Sunday school picnic! Impulsively, he dialed Doberman's extension, even though to speak directly before telling Crossley might almost smack of openness and fair play. Surely the cat was entitled to play a bit with the mouse. But when there was no answer, he left no message.

Monday morning found Stellworth, bright and early, standing in Doberman's office. A little too bright and early, as it happened, but he had brought some reading from his own office and was willing to wait. At 9:15 Doberman sauntered in, humming Beethoven's Ninth. Stellworth's ashen demeanor seemed to signal something big, but it was hard to say what. Doberman shut the door and seized the favorable vantage point of his chair, pointing Stellworth to the low-flung love seat.

For a moment they sat in silence. Stellworth, trembling with eagerness though he was, felt suddenly and unaccountably shy. It occurred to him that he hated the sight of blood, especially his own in the event that Doberman should grow desperate. Finally he mumbled that he had something to say about the Barlow case.

"Need advice?" asked Doberman. "Only too glad to help."

"But it's not exactly, or not just, about the Barlow case. I think it has some broader ramifications as well."

Doberman drummed his fingers together, looking up, however, with the open and eager expression of an unusually open and eager beaver. This further unnerved Stellworth. So, shelving a planned address on the Qualities of a Good Lawyer and the Ashby & Cinders Way, he got right to the point.

"Do you remember the brief we filed, or rather that the other guys filed last week?"

"Oh, yes. Quite a team effort."

"But the assumption of risk part was all yours."

"Someone had to do it."

"You were rather busy that weekend, as I recall. I seem to remember that you left the office early one night to go to the opera."

"Someone had to do it."

"Well, maybe you shouldn't have gone to the opera."

In reply, Doberman raised his left eyebrow three-eighths of an inch and his right eyebrow one-quarter of an inch, a combination that he had always found effective in expressing quizzical bemusement.

Stellworth plodded on. "Maybe you should have spent more time in the library."

Doberman decided to shorten the agony. "Let me guess. You've been looking at my section of the brief."

"Yes."

"You've been checking all my case citations."

"One at least."

Doberman glanced keenly at Stellworth for a moment, to make sure he wasn't giving away a still-intact secret. "You've been finding cases that were reheard and reversed just before I wrote the brief. Citations that weren't available yet when I did the research."

Stellworth goggled at this. It was just faintly possible, he thought, that Doberman was telling the truth. Shepard's citations do lag a bit at times, and the red pamphlet that Doberman had used might already have been replaced in the library by a more updated version. Even computer research through Lexis, on the dedicated terminal in one of the side carrels in the library, might have involved a lag period of several days. It would be difficult to prove that Doberman had indeed been derelict in checking the volume available to him at the time.

Then Stellworth remembered a term from his Torts class in

law school: strict liability. An individual is strictly liable for an injury if he must pay even in the absence of negligence or other fault. In the high-pressure context of a high-powered law firm, the concept seemed extremely fair to Stellworth. He knew that others in responsible positions would think it fair as well.

Accordingly, Stellworth muttered that he doubted the *Tomcat Industries* citation had not been available at the time, but that it didn't matter anyway; Doberman's responsibility was to get it right now. If Doberman felt otherwise, they could discuss the matter further in front of their elders and betters.

"You mean you're really going to tell them about it?" Doberman asked, loading the word "them" with extra topspin to express his incredulity. "How will that help?"

Stellworth tried a short, bitter laugh, which came out like a bark owing to his lack of practice.

"I mean, they're honorable men," Doberman continued. "You know what they'll have to do."

Stellworth allowed that he had a general idea.

"They'll have to correct it. You can't knowingly mislead the Commission, even if you're just of counsel. And then where will we be? The firm will lose credibility and very possibly a major client. It won't help win the case, and we'll blow our long track record of no errors in the work we send out. What's more, you'll be the one who is responsible."

"Me??!!" asked Stellworth in shock.

"Yes, you. By not having the guts to shield Crossley from knowing about it."

Again Stellworth felt taken back, but again the feeling was only temporary.

"It's going to come out anyway," he said. "Don't you remember when we get the draft reply brief?"

"Shortly before the partnership meeting." Doberman was about to add, "How like you to notice it," but in the nick of time he remembered the old gag about the pot calling the kettle black.

Then he thought of how this evil timing might help at least to buy him a breathing space. "Okay, you've got me this time. Even on the government reply brief, which I think comes out by the end of the day that Friday, you can get it messengered to Crossley if you really want to make sure he sees it on time." (Stellworth was certain to think of this anyway.) "But of course it's just one thing, and I think when they look at the whole record they'll make me a partner anyway. Still, it is going to come out; I really can't stop it. So what's the hurry? Why tell everyone now when they're certain to hear about it in due course? Who knows—it might even dilute the final impact if they hear about it sooner."

"If you really thought that, you wouldn't be trying to stop me."

This was a good point. Perhaps Doberman should just give up the fight for secrecy and turn his attention to counter-measures. Still, even if he was being self-indulgent, he wanted to keep the toothpaste in the tube for as long as he could.

"Okay, maybe that's how I should think of it, but I don't. Maybe I'm wrong. You should do what's best for you. Think of it this way. It costs you nothing to keep quiet for a bit longer, and maybe I can make it worth your while."

"How?"

"Do you remember *Der Meistersinger*? I scored pretty well with Cinders by giving him the lowdown on the performance. It was for a Friends of the Opera lunch. By now he must already have landed a client. He practically called me a rainmaker on account of this. Suppose I tell him that I was too busy and you went to the opera instead of me. You gave me the lowdown, and I simply passed it on to him."

This was potentially a high price to pay, but for now Doberman did not necessarily really propose to pay it. He was merely making a verbal offer to pay it at some point in the future. Maybe something would come up before he actually had to decide whether it was worth his while to sacrifice the credit for reporting on the opera merely in exchange for a spot of delay.

Stellworth, however, shook his head. "He'd never believe it. For one thing, why would I let you take the credit?"

"Why not? He's not the one agonizing about making partner. And he has no idea if you and I are friends or not. As far as he's concerned, we're just two associates who share a common interest in the arts."

"But I was sitting right there when you told him about the opera."

"Noblesse oblige. You had given me your word. Luckily, on reflection I'm noble too and must insist that you get fair credit."

"But I was in the office on the night of the opera."

"He'll never know that. Do you think he's going to launch an investigation?"

"How do I know you'll really tell him I'm the one who saw the opera?"

"I'll tell him in front of you."

"And all this just for not telling Crossley right away about the citation error? There's no binding quid pro quo on me?"

"That's right," said Doberman. "Take it or leave it."

Stellworth agreed to take it and withdrew. While still fearing that somehow this was a trick, it didn't seem to have a real downside. In contract terms, it was a unilateral offer by Doberman, conditioned on Stellworth's not telling anyone yet, but not actually extracting from him (in the language of the first-year Contracts course at law school) even a peppercorn of consideration before the offer was fulfilled. Come to think of it, there was really no consideration after fulfillment either, so it wasn't really a contract at all: just a statement of present intention that might conceivably modify how Stellworth, of his own continuing free will, decided to act. What could be the harm in being swayed by that?

Doberman gave a deep sigh once the coast was clear. Now

what, he asked himself. He had bought some time at zero cost, at least for as long as he could evade a three-way meeting with Stellworth and Cinders. Then, even if he didn't keep his word, he would be no worse off than before. Still, the situation remained critical.

It was about to get more critical. Doberman's secretary buzzed to tell him that Cinders' secretary was on the line. Cinders wanted to see him immediately. He should be careful; Cinders was angry.

14. Red Roses for a Blue Lady

Angry? Cinders? What about the beautiful friendship that he and Doberman had been nurturing?

Perhaps the new client at the Friends of the Opera meeting had fallen through. But, if so, whose fault was that: the fisherman, or the poor schnook from the bait and tackle shop who offered him a worm?

Whatever the problem, Doberman could tell it was bad when he arrived at the inner sanctum. Cinders was on the phone, of course, but in place of his usual obliviousness he spared Doberman an angry glance and motioned him imperiously into a chair. Then, after completing the phone call, Cinders buzzed his secretary and actually told her to hold all of his calls for five minutes.

"Friends of the Opera last Friday," he began. Doberman decided to wait for a verb.

"We were talking about *Der Meistersinger*. They ate up what I said about Traversi. But when I started criticizing Luga I found out that she missed the performance."

"She what?!?"

"I gather the understudy was clearly announced at the

start. People groaned a bit. And even if you weren't listening, anyone who follows opera should have known immediately that she wasn't the singer. Or so I was given to believe, if not in so many words."

Poor Cinders, Doberman thought for a second, his sympathy extending most readily to the powerful. That must have been embarrassing. But more to the point, poor Doberman. How could Gidget have failed to notice and alert him? Was she deaf, dumb, and blind?

Meanwhile, the old boy's eyes were boring into him, the great white-maned head cocked slightly to the side. Then suddenly Doberman had an inspiration—a desperate and pitiful one, to be sure, but at the moment the best available.

"That's incredible!" he said. "You'd have to be a dunce to think it was Luga when it wasn't."

There was an awkward pause.

"By you I don't mean *you*, of course. I mean, if someone went to the opera and couldn't tell that it wasn't Luga they'd have to be a, an ignoramus. A philistine."

Still Cinders kept silent. He was wondering if this could this be a breakdown, a bizarre, bare-all confession of inadequacy. One should never own up to such failings publicly; it was unprofessional.

Doberman moved briskly to the punchline. "And that's why I'm really surprised and disappointed in STELLWORTH. Sure, his taste in art is a bit stolid. One wonders if he can really appreciate intense food seasoning. But surely he can go to an opera and tell the great Teresa Luga from an understudy. Or so I would have said until now."

For a moment, Cinders wondered if he had mixed up the associates. It got harder each year to tell apart all these eager young faces with their gray three-piece suits, yellow or red ties, yellow legal pads, and continual air of deference. But this time he was pretty sure.

"I sent *you* to the opera. I remember it."

"I know. And I was looking forward to it. But at the last moment I had a medical emergency. So I asked Stellworth to cover for me, and until now I thought he'd done a good job."

"You say Stellworth went. I don't recall you telling me that Stellworth liked Traversi and didn't like Luga. I definitely got the impression that it was straight from the horse's mouth."

Doberman smiled. "I was going to get around to it."

Cinders shook his head. "I'm afraid I don't believe you. You said you had gone to the opera, and you did. I can read people. I'm a poker player.

"Anyway, no lawyer in this firm would go around passing off a colleague's opinions as his own. We don't operate that way. It would probably be worse if I did believe you.

"I know you're up for partner soon. It's a tough time to make a mistake. But we're a professional business here. Strict liability."

Right on cue Cinders' buzzer rang to announce a phone call, and Doberman was dismissed. He would have felt even worse had he known that, within the half hour, Cinders would be summoning Stellworth as his arm candy for a modern art opening - strictly speaking, it was going to be photography - on an upcoming Friday night. Even in the darkest times Doberman had always held the edge on modern art, Stellworth being handicapped by his air of a barely suppressed snort when he saw anything too nearly cutting-edge or provocative.

Stellworth, as he sat at his desk absorbing the phoned invitation from Cinders' secretary, felt almost as if he were shuttling from sauna to fjord and back again like a frolicking Finn. He would flush red in the temples as he pondered the possibility that Doberman had already kept his part of the bargain and was reaping the evil fruits. Then would come an icy chill next to his armpits as Stellworth imagined what the art at the opening would be like. Graffiti was being called art these days, as he painfully remembered from a recent experience, and he had heard ugly rumors about even worse.

The photographer's name, Mapplethorpe, sounded familiar but he could not quite place it.

Then he would flash both hot and cold again as he contemplated tattling to Crossley immediately. This was actually consistent with the strict terms of the bargain if Doberman had already performed. But if not, the bargain was perhaps no longer necessary. Stellworth was now such an evident favorite with Cinders that being linked with Doberman in any way might even at this point be unseemly.

Stellworth did not really relish a pitched fight in front of Crossley at this juncture, however. Fights were too exhausting and distasteful, unless he could feel in his arteries the rage and zeal of his Crusading ancestors as they catapulted the severed heads of captured spies over the battlements of besieged castles. No such steely emotions consumed him now, however – the hot and cold flashes were too disorienting – and he decided that the tattling could wait. Delay would cost him nothing now anyway. Even after the opening, he would still have plenty of time before the climactic P-day.

Calmed by this resolution, Stellworth might have cackled like a stage villain and pulled leeringly at his long moustachios if his parents had taught him that this was how the better sort of people behave. Instead, he gave a short sniff, straightened his tie, and headed to the coffee room. Perhaps half-decaf this time; he was getting jumpy.

Doberman, meanwhile, was sitting at his desk with a yellow legal pad, compulsively drawing crisp little cubes and pyramids as he weighed considerations too sensitive to be written down on lists. Who knew who might search his trash? For all the body blows that this evil day had brought, he was starting to feel like Marechale Foch at the Battle of the Marne. "My center is crumbling? My right is retreating? Situation excellent – I attack!"

On the Barlow and Cinders fronts, he must for now stay hunkered in the trenches. Perhaps the enemy would sweep too far and in due course invite counter-encirclement. But there was one feasible current initiative: rapprochement with Lyla, actually a kind of attack to the rear to secure his escape route if needed. He had been thinking he might let her stew for a while, perhaps even past the partnership meeting, but now a marriage proposal in advance of any bad news on that front - even well-founded rumors that he was in trouble - seemed advisable. She would probably accept him in any event, but he did not want to have to plead with her, or be suspected of feeling a true anxiety about her answer that he would rather smirkingly feign.

Then there was the delicate situation concerning her father at Carp, Stone & Tyler. This might be an actual deal-breaker if Lyla suspected that he was proposing marriage as a way of securing a fallback job. But she would never suspect him if he proposed while she still thought that he thought that he was certain of making it.

Doberman swiftly began thinking through the reconciliation. Today was Monday, April 18. The partnership meeting was scheduled for Friday, May 13. Twenty-five days to go, or call it three and a half weeks. So he needed to have Lyla back by May 12, but that was bound to be a funky time, and also one that offered no allowance for slippage.

So suppose he pushed it forward a week to Friday, May 6. Even that seemed a bit tight. Perhaps, then, he should aim to reconcile with her no later than Friday, April 29, eleven days from now. Last night he would have said that this was far too sudden, but surely he could make it work.

Indeed, at the moment eleven days felt like an eternity. To feel better about the Cinders situation, he needed to create some sense of accomplishment immediately. This itch or thirst to act could possibly be dangerous. Perhaps he should placate it by acting immediately, but merely in setting things up for the future, without risking an irreversible error in judgment.

On his way home, therefore, Doberman stopped by a florist

and arranged for a single red rose to go to Lyla's apartment for four straight nights, starting next Monday, that would be the 25th. He also reluctantly shelved his plan to tell Gidget that he had broken up with Lyla and could now start seeing her openly. Instead, she would immediately get a dozen red roses in a single shipment, with a note saying "Thank you for New York – It was great – I'll call you by the end of the week."

For the rest of the week and well into the next one, he was careful to steer clear of both women. He did, in keeping with his promise, give Gidget an amorous phone call at her home on Friday night. But he said goodbye without promising anything more definite than to call her again, and hopefully (but no promises) to see her at the end of the next week. Things were bound to get cleared up soon, he said, but for the moment they both just needed to be patient.

Sleeping alone at home each night, for an entire week and well into the next, was a novel experience for Doberman. Every now and then he considered making a bid for excitement, perhaps at some local watering hole like the Sign of the Whale where he had experienced furtive success in the past. But he never felt quite tempted enough to ask himself seriously whether this would be a good idea. The fact that he was now on the wrong side of thirty must mean something after all. At least he got plenty of sleep.

Finally, late on the afternoon of Thursday the 28th, having softened up (he hoped) Lyla with a red rose for three straight nights and with one more to come, he called her at work to propose dinner at six o'clock in a Chinese restaurant near the office. She was out, but he left the invitation anyway in a cryptic message. Within the hour, she had called back while he was out and left an equally cryptic message accepting.

He arrived at the restaurant eight minutes late, having guessed correctly that under the circumstances she would relax her usual promptness and arrive no more than five minutes late. She was sitting with a just-poured Chinese beer, her lips pursed tensely.

"How are you, Lyla?" he asked as he sat down across from her, sounding glib yet with a little catch in the throat that he had practiced in the morning.

Lyla mumbled "Okay," and asked how he was doing.

Doberman shrugged, hoping to appear neither happy, which would be inapposite, or too sad, which might start her thinking that she could dictate the terms for a renewal of relations. This was followed by several seconds of silence.

"Nice weather we're having," he said finally.

"Although it did rain this morning."

"Yes, it did."

Another impasse. All too often the weather leaves no place to go.

"Is this place okay?" he asked her. It was an occasional lunch site for people from Ashby & Cinders, known more for speed than quality.

"Yeah."

"The place by my house is much better, but I didn't know if you'd want to go there."

Lyla was looking at him more intently now, and he took her hand between his own two. "I'm glad we're still friends," he said.

"Me too."

But, in lieu of following up immediately, he led the conversation to old times, and then gradually to the lighter side of current office politics. In the edited version, the citation error was provably not his fault because the rehearing post-dated the brief, and he remained Cinders' fair-haired boy.

At length Lyla asked him, leaning forward slightly, her eyes shining, whether he thought he was going to make it.

"Make partner?" He smiled, he hoped inscrutably. "I'm not worried. I'd say I'm confident. Cautiously confident. You can never really be much more than that."

"I'd vote for you. But sometimes I think you should be more careful. You sometimes have a way of getting people angry, and I don't just mean me. And sometimes people take these things to heart more than you do, or for longer."

Doberman nodded sagely. True or not, he did not especially like hearing it.

Talking as they were about Doberman, a subject of interest to them both, the time passed quickly. When the check came, he offered to take her home.

"Oh, that's not necessary."

"My pleasure," he insisted, and she subsided while he hailed a cab.

All the way home, Lyla was wondering if she wanted to invite him in (her mother would be out), and, almost as a distinct question, whether in fact she would do so. The issue was bound to be posed soon, since a man of his caliber, when offering to take someone home, could scarcely have intended a mere single entendre.

When they arrived at her door, however, Doberman simply shook her hand, kissed her solemnly on the cheek, and offered his best impression of a soulful glance. "Enjoy the rose," he said; it had been lying in front of the door wrapped in paper. Then he turned on his heel and retreated down the hallway.

This decided things. Lyla called him back with a cry and embraced him passionately. "I'm so sorry," she said, but he was entirely gracious. In her bedroom later, as they lay together feeling a warmer glow than they had known for some time, he suddenly excused himself to run naked into the living room, where he had left his suit jacket. Fortunately, Mother, after noisily puttering about upon her return, had retired for the night. He returned, clutching and imperfectly concealing the little black box that she had seen in his hand once before.

"There's something they give you in the hospital just before surgery." he said. "I think it's called Versid. It causes amnesia but going back a bit, not just forward. I remember getting it when I had my hernia operation. Remember I told you that I went blank right when they said they were going to knock me out because the local wasn't working? Even though I couldn't have really been knocked out for a couple of minutes afterward? That was Versid."

Lyla nodded.

He opened his hand and offered the box. "This is my Versid for you. Let's just forget about that Sunday, and agree from now on that it never happened ... Will you marry me?"

"Of course I will. But I'm glad the Sunday thing happened. I didn't trust you enough. I've learned. But I was feeling unappreciated. Maybe that's why I was so jealous. I think we both have to do a better job from now on if this is going to work."

She isn't stupid, Doberman thought. Thank goodness she's so off-kilter right now. I'll have to be careful with her, but I guess I always knew that.

There also remained Gidget to consider. She might prove to be a hot potato before she was done, and he was still feeling the heat, too.

15. I Know It When I See It

Lyla expected handling Mother on Friday morning to be the most ticklish part of things. How would she greet Doberman, and for that matter would she even to deign to greet him? What would she say when she noticed the engagement ring?

Ever since Monday, Mom had been sneering at Doberman's red roses. Earlier still, she had harumphed when Lyla told her that the story with Bill was much more complicated than she realized, and that he had adequately explained his trip to New York notwithstanding their breakup in the lounge at National Airport.

"This I've got to hear," Mom had said the first time. "What did he say?"

"I'm still not ready for this conversation," Lyla had replied, firmly enough to make her subside.

If only they had possessed flash cards to signal and reinforce their mutually well-known sentiments, the interchange could have gone a bit further. Mom could have held up Card 14, standing for "I just don't want to see you get hurt." Or else maybe Card 23, meaning "You can't trust men; at least, not this one." And Lyla could have responded with Card 6 ("I know what I'm doing"), or else Card 21 ("You should have more confidence in me"), or perhaps even the rarely-played Card 52 ("Please keep your bitterness to yourself").

They had not wanted actually to say any of these things in words, however, and in any event it would have been superfluous. The whole set of exchanges did not really even require so much as cue cards, at least from the standpoint of informing either of them about the other's thoughts.

As it happened on this Friday morning, Mom decided to make things easier by rising for an early breakfast and heading out. Lyla proudly wore her diamond ring to breakfast anyway, but by the time she and Doberman left for work it was back in her desk drawer.

"Let's definitely go to work together," he had suggested. "Let people know we're back as a couple, or at least not act like it's a secret. But the engagement ... this is just the wrong time. I'd hate to rock the boat so publicly, like I'm panicking or something, so close to the partnership decision."

Lyla docilely agreed. The only person she told about the engagement was Mom, in a late-morning telephone call from her office. Mom was surprised and even, after a moment's pause, congratulatory, but evidently not prepared to share her thoughts. No doubt this was just as well. At the office, Lyla kept to herself throughout the day, and left at five on the strength of Doberman's pledges to call her when he could, and hopefully to see her after working late. He had also surreptitiously left word with Gidget to stick around past five. Once Lyla was safely out the door, he summoned her.

Gidget poked her head in the door of Doberman's office, but without coming in. "Can we go somewhere?" she asked.

"I thought we could just have a little talk, maybe here."

"A talk. That sounds grim."

"I don't know. It's great to see you." He was feeling irresolute.

"Can we go to your place? Or at least a bar?"

He shook his head. "I've got to stay here." Then suddenly a mischievous thought seized him. All this caution was so boring anyway.

"I saw Crossley leaving for the night. He has a great office, and it's pretty far from the library. Kind of in Partner's Row, which is a ghost town on Friday nights. Why don't we meet there in half an hour?"

Doberman spent the half hour working on rogs (litigators' lingo for interrogatories), and arrived promptly to find Gidget pretending to check some files in the hallway cabinet. They entered Crossley's office, and he locked the door.

"Look at this place," he said. "This is the best view, short of the top five partners, in the whole place. I'd love to get something like this."

"Or maybe something like this?" With a single smooth motion, Gidget pulled her dress over her head. Then she reached for his belt with one hand, a finger from her other hand at her lips. "No words," she said.

Soon their bodies were in motion, flat on the carpet. They would have been interested to know that, within a few minutes, another body was also in motion, decidedly perpendicular and headed their way.

Crossley, having forgotten some documents that he wanted to scan over the weekend and with downtown plans for the evening anyway, had left home ahead of Anne, who would be picking him up at the corner of 16th and K Streets in her car. Just now he had alit from the Metro two blocks south. He was headed for the office, his wingtips echoing on the pavement like messengers of doom. Or perhaps not, since they were soft-soled for maximum comfort.

Crossley was in a state of gloomy introspection. He always liked the end of the week, except that it meant the start of the weekend. Right now he was dreading dinner. The other couple would be Jim and Jill Hankins, the couple from Anne's parents' country house a few weekends earlier. Jim was by now apparently a lock for a high job at the Democratic National Committee. Thus, so long as former Vice President Mondale got the Democratic nomination next year as expected, he was certain to play an important role in the campaign and perhaps beyond. The apparently developing intimacy with someone of such great Washington status made Crossley feel anxious, a bit after the fashion of a pimply teenager who is thinking of asking the prom queen to go to a drive-in movie with him.

"Don't worry about it," Anne had insisted. "He liked you the other weekend. You're an interesting animal to him - an actual lawyer lawyer, as opposed to a political or government lawyer. "

Crossley had nodded glumly.

"And another thing," Anne had said. "Besides remembering to play up the downtown lawyer bit. Stay calm and reserved. Sometimes when you're nervous you start to babble. And keep in mind, this guy doesn't expect you to know all the political inside dope."

Well, maybe it would be okay. The point about the babbling was actually a good one. With people he wanted to impress, Crossley could find it hard to stop once he got started, even if he could see that he was not doing well. But he also had the upcoming partnership meeting to brood about. The stuff about who made partner should be fun, but the annual battle over dividing the spoils considerably less so. How many "points" could he successfully claim for purposes of maximizing his share of the partnership draw when he was generally more of an errand boy, servicing the senior partners' clients, than the maestro of his own?

One matter at least had played out in a sense better than expected, although in another sense worse. This was the Barlow case, in which the client was evidently very pleased with the contribution that the firm, or more specifically he and his minions, had been able to serve up so swiftly. The fact that, at the reply brief stage, Ashby & Cinders would get to review and comment on Nesson & Wesson's work before it was submitted was already a compliment, albeit well short of total victory. There could be further payoffs down the road, such as the lead role in district court litigation with the FPHC if the commissioners upheld the enforcement arm.

More importantly, however, the Barlow people had been hinting at their view that Ashby & Cinders, and he in particular as the managing partner, might have a real knack for complex and politically sensitive administrative proceedings. There was a matter in Alaska, involving pipeline discharge that was suspected of causing environmental damage and a suite of worker illnesses, that several state agencies were competing to commandeer. Local counsel would do much of the legwork, but Barlow Industries was beginning to doubt that they could man the controls properly. This called for top-flight Washington counsel with extensive federal regulatory experience.

Crossley could bring this up at the partnership meeting as an instance of rainmaking that really was attributable to him, notwithstanding that Barlow Industries was an old Cinders client. Actually handling the pipeline case would be another matter, however. It might call for frequent trips to Alaska, and even some stays there for several days at a time. Crossley hated cold winters and had heard horrible tales about the bloodthirsty mosquitoes that haunt Alaska's summers. Plus, it was unlikely that he could take many associates with him. Riding herd (or trying to) over local counsel that would have preferred to get the lead role would be considerably less fun than looking over the shoulders of subordinates.

Arriving at his office, Crossley was surprised to find the door closed. He reached for the handle, but it was locked. He was about to take out his key when he realized there were sounds coming from the inside.

Doberman and Gidget had subsided and were now in earnest conversation, little above a whisper. Crossley could tell it was a man and woman, but he could not identify them or make out most of the words.

It was demeaning for him to stand there with his ear to the door. Still, no one else was around, and some of the words were clear enough.

Come to think of it, given what he could surmise about the activities inside, this was also a bit more exciting than anything else he had planned at the moment. He hadn't even gotten to paw through a dirty magazine since the time his first wife, early in their relationship, had forced him to ditch his entire collection. Who knew - maybe the couple would start up again. Although increasingly it didn't seem to be going that way.

"I can't do this any more," came from the man. Also, "I feel like I could love you but," something or other, then something about a bad time. Also, "you can't imagine how much I know you" – or was it "owe you"? – and, several times, "my feelings."

From the woman, interspersed with the above, came something about being surprised or maybe not surprised. More likely the latter, because then, more clearly, "I expected this." She sounded like she was bearing up pretty well; certainly there was nothing approaching tears.

Who were they? He burned to know but feared to show himself, especially now that he had been lurking for several minutes like a stranger in the bushes. Prurience yielded to temper as he started to consider the disrespect of these people – perhaps from the mailroom? – coming in and using his office this way. Unless, of course, it was a senior partner, but the voices sounded too young.

They had to be from the mailroom, at least the man. Probably the woman was someone from the outside. Crossley was intimidated by the mailroom guys, who tended to have longish hair and even tattoos. They distantly reminded him of kids named Sal or Vinnie who used to beat him up occasionally in junior high school. But maybe that was unfair. The mailroom guys were gentler, more in the Springsteen or reggae than the greaser mode. Did Springsteen and reggae fandom go together? He couldn't remember. But anyway, the mailroom guys were prone at worst to understated derision, surely not to violence, although sometimes a whiff of derision was bad enough.

Then he heard rustling sounds, maybe the couple's clothing coming off or on. He was just deciding that perhaps it would be prudent to flee when he heard their footsteps coming quickly towards the door and it swung open.

It would be hard to say who was most shocked. To Gidget, it was just an embarrassing moment, but rather an excruciating one, and at a point when she wanted to sit down in privacy and reflect for a few minutes about what had happened. She felt kicked in the stomach but also half-relieved, and maybe in the long run more glad than sad that the whole thing had happened.

Doberman simply could not believe that Crossley was standing there in front of him. What else could go wrong now? How could the gods be so unfair to him? Then again, might Crossley be as anxious as he was to pretend afterwards that this had never happened? Maybe this would all seem funny some day.

Crossley, as shamefaced as if he were the wrongdoer, was angry to be feeling that way. Doberman was taking his fancy to this office entirely too far! What was he going to do next – spend the night on the sofa? Urinate on the desk?

Doberman decided to brazen it out. "Miss O'Malley was just taking some dictation from me. Rogs. My secretary's gone for the day. I thought this was a quiet spot where I could concentrate." But he winked before heading down the hall, several strides behind Gidget and making no effort to catch up with her.

Crossley put his hand to his forehead. Could he have

imagined all this? Was there any chance, no matter how small, that Doberman was telling the truth? Then he noticed a small wet spot in the center of the carpet. He stumbled to his desk, gathered up the needed papers, and fled as fast as he could.

By the time he got downstairs, Anne was waiting out front in the car.

"You're pale," she said.

"It's nothing."

"Are you feeling okay?"

"I'm fine. Let's just go to dinner."

At dinner, Crossley had little to say and seemed distracted. But he did have enough sense to give himself some cover by telling everybody that a heavy deal was going down at the office. He couldn't really talk about it, but it might be big. Even page three of the Washington Post big.

"It's good you could come to dinner anyway," Anne put in loyally.

"Well, I wanted to," he said, a bit tonelessly but hoping to pass muster under the circumstances.

"What was all that about?" she asked him later as they headed home.

"Do you think they bought what I said about the big deal going down?"

"I would think so - I bought it."

"Well, it was made up. There's just some stuff going on with uppity associates. You know, they get near partnership and seem to forget everything. You don't really need the details."

"Okay. Well, the good news is, Jim really likes you. While you were in the bathroom he was trying to get me to say what the big deal was about, and he laughed when I said I had no idea. I told you're really serious about attorney-client privilege. He said, 'I didn't know they made guys like that any more.' I told you he'd be a sucker for a lawyer lawyer."

Crossley was not the only Ashby & Cinders lawyer to have a spectatorial experience that bordered on the pornographic this

Friday night. Ordinarily, no doubt he would have been. These were not, after all, people generally engaged in re-enacting Guccione's *Caligula*, or even in seeking it at the video store. But this was the night of the Mapplethorpe show. At 6:41 sharp, only moments after Crossley had staggered dazedly out of the building, Stellworth snapped shut his briefcase and took the elevator to the basement. Cinders had told him to present himself at 6:45, at the elevator entrance to the building's underground garage.

They would be taking the firm's limo to the show, no less. Stellworth had never ridden in it before, and probably half the firm's partners hadn't either. It was entirely the plaything of the two name partners, who nonetheless made all the partners pay for it. Stellworth had overheard a couple of them grumbling about this, although no doubt they would never bring it up officially and would be thrilled enough if they got a ride every few years.

All day long, Stellworth had been trying to place the name of the artist whose work they would be seeing. In a game of free association, he would have been inclined to say: "Mapplethorpe? – Scandal." But just what the scandal was about, he could not remember. Maybe the man had blasphemed the Catholic Church or punched out a critic.

As they rode to the gallery, Cinders warned him to expect something risqué. "But we need to be broadminded about it, and certainly not look uncomfortable; that would be provincial. If you can't think of anything else to say, praise how the photographs are lit, or say that you like the composition."

Inside the door they met an acquaintance or friend of Cinders.

"Lowell is one of our rising young stars," Cinders explained as he made the introductions. "Paul Woodson is a Friend of the Opera and he also runs a few companies. You may have heard of him."

Stellworth tried to nod knowingly.

"Is Lowell here a Luga expert, too?" Woodson asked. He seemed to think this was funny, although Stellworth could not quite see why and Cinders evidently did not find it so either.

They arrived at a small anteroom in which two large-scale photographs were displayed. Stellworth looked up and blanched. In the first a naked man was thrusting out his oversized genitals. The man in the second photo was dressed to a point, but with an open fly through which he was exposing himself.

Stellworth quickly turned away from the display wall to examine the crowd. Extremely well-dressed people, the men in dark suits and the women in their jewelry, were studying the photos with a kind of studiedly casual intensity, as if they were just watching paint dry but had a keen professorial interest in the process.

Woodson nudged him and asked: "What do you think?"

Stellworth turned to face the first photograph. "I, the, it's very well composed. I think the lighting is very clear."

"Well, I think it's disgusting," Woodson replied. "I'll look at the whole show and not say anything because I don't want to make a fool of myself, but that doesn't mean I have to like it."

Cinders raised an eyebrow an eighth of an inch, and Stellworth had the feeling of having flunked a test, even though he had done exactly as told.

They entered the next room. Here it was full shock treatment. The photographs splayed on the walls seemed to be sprouting penises, or was it penes, everywhere that Stellworth looked. Sometimes a nude photograph was cut off at the knees and the head, as if no other body parts mattered. The full-body shots showed men embracing and kissing each other. Many of the men were heavily tattooed, and some appeared to be mutilated.

Another man came up and shook Cinders' hand. Again there were gracious introductions, although Stellworth was by now too dazed to catch the other man's name or what he did.

"What do you think?" the man asked Stellworth.

No more hypocrisy, he thought; it doesn't even pay.

"I find it pretty revolting," he said. "If this is art, then I – well – I'll just leave it at that."

The man raised both eyebrows and turned to Cinders. "Your young friend here seems to be having a hard time. What do you think?"

"Well, you know me. I'm an old fogy. This isn't my style. But I can appreciate the composition. It's very controlled. The contrast and definition are very interesting – almost Renaissance, I'd say."

The man nodded and moved on. Cinders startled Stellworth by suddenly grabbing his wrist and squeezing hard.

"Do you have to embarrass me in front of the director of the gallery?"

"I, I thought I would be honest. Woodson didn't like it when I talked about the composition."

"You've got to have a little more finesse than that. Paul's a conservative man, I would have thought you could see that. But if you're going to tell the director of a major gallery that you hate his show – which I just did, by the way – you have to know how to say it."

Stellworth just looked down at the floor, which at least was a pornography-free zone. He started silently counting to a hundred, then five hundred and over again, waiting for the moment when he would be free to leave. Cinders, by his side, was circulating suavely but largely ignoring him.

As they went at last to fetch their coats, Stellworth made a desperate effort to retrieve the ground he knew he had lost.

"I guess I'm not a modern art person," he said. "But I do know opera." And then, with a stab at a casual air, "Presumably you know I'm the one who went to *Der Meistersinger* for you.

Doberman couldn't go at the last minute, so I covered it for him and filled him in. He must have mentioned it."

Stellworth was thinking: So much the better if he hasn't told you yet.

To his shock, however, Cinders scowled back at him. "So you're the idiot who didn't know about the understudy! Doberman said it was you but I didn't believe him!"

Stellworth stood openmouthed. This was treachery beyond imagination. One could hardly blame him for not realizing that Doberman had at least initially made the opera offer in a kind of technical good faith. (He had only meant to renege on this offer down the road, rather than realizing it was a poison pill.) Doberman would no doubt have understood that such misunderstandings and misattributions of malice are the hazards of war. Similarly, if you are Jack the Ripper, you simply take the chance of being blamed each time your presence is detected near the scene of a ghoulish murder, even if some of them are not your handiwork.

Once Stellworth had escaped from the area, to yell "Fie!" and "Drat!" was the work of an instant. Revenge was slower, but not by much. On Saturday morning he called Crossley at home to report on Doberman's citation error in the Barlow case. Crossley seemed to find the news quite interesting, and promised to set up a showdown meeting at the office on Monday morning.

It was lucky for Stellworth that he had this showdown to look forward to all weekend. Otherwise, he would have felt grim indeed. The lingering stench of the Friday night calamity with Cinders was hard to bear even with the knowledge that someone else would soon enough be getting his comeuppance. (How could Doberman possibly, in a thousand years, wriggle out of this one?)

Making things worse, this was the long-scheduled weekend when Stellworth's parents would be making their annual visit to Washington. Of course they had insisted on staying in the guest bedroom. Or more precisely, they had just assumed this would be the arrangement without ever asking if it was best, even though they could easily have afforded a hotel.

Normally, Stellworth didn't mind his parents, even though he had little to say to them. Certainly they fit well enough the Central Casting requirements that he would have envisioned for the parts, aside perhaps from his mother being slightly the taller of the two. Slim and distinguished with jacket and tie for the one; prim and crisply turned out if physically a bit large for a woman and almost a bit ungainly for the other. Especially from a distance and in short encounters, they were entirely presentable.

This was a bad time for the visit, however, given not only all the approaching partnership verdict but also their recently intensified campaign for grandchildren. So long as Stellworth's sisters had no marriage plans or even eligible candidates on the horizon, which so far as he knew was still the current state of affairs, he was bound to bear the brunt of this campaign.

Stellworth could imagine circumstances in which he would want to have a child, preferably a son. Just one, he thought, a solo just as he had been until he reached age six and the first of his sisters was born. But it was hard to say when he would want a child, even if he made partner and things eased up at the office. The children he saw from time to time could be noisy or smelly or rude even if their parents made some show of trying to keep them in order, which not all of them did. Some of the scenes he had witnessed on airplanes and in restaurants …

Sarah could envision having a baby in the house more easily than he could, at least if they had a lot of help. But she didn't feel she could countenance a pregnancy. With the summer approaching, it tired her even to think of all the heavy, sweaty, staggering women she had seen from time to time with their distended stomachs, sometimes eating the most disgusting things.

At dinner with his parents on Saturday night, when the subject finally came up, Stellworth and Sarah tried to tell them about the reasons for what they called their "hesitation" on this front. Both of them were so busy already, pregnancy is so tough, babies and young children are so tough.

"You're not planning to adopt?" his mother asked fearfully.

Of course not, and, although Stellworth did not say so, the very suggestion felt insulting, as if he did not know enough to value the blood.

Nonetheless, his father chimed in. "There was an article in the *Globe* last Sunday about Vietnamese boat children. You know a lot of them were adopted by American families. Now, a few years out, quite a few have turned out to have real problems."

Stellworth caught Sarah's eye and winced, but chose not to say anything.

"If you're worried about paying for childcare," his mother said, "we can help. Can't we?"

She looked to his father for confirmation, which he gave with a curt nod. But this was more insulting still.

"Lawyers are well paid, you know," Stellworth said. There were plenty in the family, so they already ought to know this.

But this only brought them to the other sore point. His parents knew that he was up for partnership shortly, and naturally wanted a fuller picture. Father was an architect, so he didn't really know law firms from the inside, but his older brother was a senior partner in the old-line Boston firm where Stellworth's grandfather had practiced before. So far as Father understood law firms, at least from the old days, they simply hired the right people out of law school, and after that it was all smooth sailing. Leaving aside, of course, the occasional odd misfit or black sheep who drank too much or wanted to travel.

Stellworth tried to explain that things didn't really work that way any more.

"I know," his father said. "Everything's changed. David's firm" - this was the elder brother - "hires Catholics and Jews these days. They've been doing it for about ten years. Some of them work out really well. And apparently they're about to get a black fellow."

"Yes. There's no more prejudice, and that's fine with me. We live in a different world now than when Gramps or even Uncle David were coming up. But the thing that really has changed for the worse is the personality types. Some of the people you get in law firms these days …"

Here his mother cut in. "You know what your father always says. It isn't personality that wins the day. It's character."

Both parents looked rather pleased with this saying, but Stellworth and even Sarah had heard it a few hundred times before.

"You're going to make partner, aren't you?" his mother asked suddenly, an anxious note in her voice.

Stellworth shrugged, he hoped with enough of the Ronald Colman spirit. I'd better, he told himself. My parents will never understand it if I don't. Which is not to say they'll really understand it even if I do.

16. Trojan Horse Strategy

All rogged out, was how Doberman had described himself to Lyla on that same Friday night when, after his encounters with Gidget and Crossley, he had called to put off seeing her until Saturday morning. In the wake of their latest reconciliation, he figured to have a few free passes before she began closely scrutinizing him again. They spent a quiet weekend together, interrupted only by the odd four hours here and two there when he needed to be at work.

Doris, apart from raising an eyebrow when Lyla told her about the Friday night cancellation, was on her best behavior. Her comportment towards Doberman was generally civil if not warm, and she did shake his hand to congratulate him on the engagement.

"You've got a firm handshake," he said.

"You've got a great young woman," she replied. "I know that you - well, yes ..." and she just trailed off.

When at the office during the weekend, Doberman spent his time holed up in his cubicle, without parading through the halls as usual. He really didn't need to prove his hours so visibly at this point, and anyway it felt like a good time to lie low. So he saw almost no one. On Monday morning, however, he arrived to find Stellworth lurking by his door.

"Lowell! Two Mondays in a row! I'm beginning to think you sometimes miss me."

"Not yet. But maybe soon. Have you checked your messages today?"

"I haven't even sat down yet."

"There should be one from Crossley, or else you'll be hearing from him presently."

Doberman froze in mid-stride for a second before resuming his saunter through the door. Crossley and Stellworth had evidently been talking. The timing was certainly interesting. There are no coincidences in foxholes; hence, they must have been discussing the Friday night Gidget episode. This was possibly bad news; the saga could hurt him on several fronts.

Perhaps Crossley had run into Stellworth later on Friday night, still so shaken that he just blurted the whole thing out. It was not his usual policy, after all, to share information with subordinates other than on a strict need-to-know basis.

"Crossley told you he was going to call me?" Doberman was pretty sure he had it figured out, but saw no reason not to probe a bit.

"Yes. He thought what we discussed was pretty serious."

We? Doberman thought. I certainly never discussed my sex life with Stellworth. But then, wedded to the assumption that Gidget, not *Tomcat Industries*, was the topic of the moment, he decided that "we" must mean Stellworth and Crossley.

"That's incredible," he said, trying to sputter a bit. "It was just a little – you and he really talked about it?"

"Yes. Why shouldn't we?"

"Why shouldn't you? What about – well, some things are personal and private. If they don't matter professionally, they shouldn't be discussed."

"You really think it doesn't matter? Crossley should just

forget about it? That's even more unprofessional than I would have expected from you."

Doberman squinted slightly and cocked his head to the side. "I still don't understand your involvement in this. And anyway Crossley didn't see anything."

"He didn't have to see it. I explained the whole thing to him."

This was stranger still. Was Stellworth giving Crossley pointers about the birds and the bees?

"*You* explained it?"

"Of course I did. You shouldn't be too surprised after that trick you pulled on me over *Der Meistersinger*." And, with an indignant snort, Stellworth stalked out.

Doberman grinned. The scene with Cinders would have been fun to witness, he thought. Better still, in bringing it to light Stellworth had committed a serious intelligence blunder. Doberman might not otherwise have learned any time soon that Cinders was once again a potential ally.

Talk about unprofessional! Catchers don't tell hitters, "That curveball off the plate was just to set you up for the fastball inside." The D-Day invasion wouldn't have gotten very far if Eisenhower had told the Germans, "We don't really like Calais as a landing site." The Russians would never have stolen the A-bomb formula if ... but suddenly Doberman looked up to see Lyla standing in front of him.

"Bill," she said, "there's something I wanted to tell you about. I was on the verge of mentioning it all weekend, but I just couldn't find the right time. I didn't want it to slide all the way to the end of the week, and I realize how stressed you could start getting, the closer we get to you know what."

"The wedding? We don't even have a date yet."

"No, the partnership meeting."

Doberman gave a gracious shrug to indicate she should continue.

"You know about my dad. Now that we're engaged I feel like you should meet him."

"Okay."

"You know I'm still angry at him; he hasn't been a very good dad. But now that we might have kids some day, I feel like we should start to bring him back in."

"Okay."

"I might have told you once he was a lawyer. He's actually still practicing, and maybe you've heard of him."

"Is that so?"

"He's at Carp, Stone & Tyler. In fact, he's Tyler."

"That's interesting. Decent enough firm. They do industrial litigation. I might have gone up against them once or twice. Never met him, of course. This *is* a surprise."

He sure doesn't sound surprised, Lyla found herself thinking. That whole speech came out a little fast. Still, if he knew about it, why should he care if I knew that he knew?

Just then Doberman's phone rang. Crossley wanted to see him immediately. He frowned, excused himself, and exited.

That doesn't look too good, Lyla thought. And suddenly she had an idea why Doberman might want to play dumb with her. Carp, Stone & Tyler was a second-tier firm but, as he had said, decent enough. He'd sneer at it if he made partner, but what if he didn't? He certainly hadn't looked too pleased when Crossley summoned him a moment ago.

Could this be why he had gotten engaged to her after all this time? Surely not; that would be stooping too low even for him. (Her love was not after all entirely blind.) What if it was the reason, however? That would be a terrible thing.

But he was going to make partner here. He expected to, and probably he knew. Most of the office scuttlebutt about him seemed to be positive. People treated him as if they thought he might be around for a while.

Even if he could stoop so low under the right circumstances, surely he was doing too well at present. He wouldn't get engaged to her just as a long-shot insurance policy unless he really wanted to; if nothing else he had guts. Lyla decided to put the entire possibility out of mind.

Up a floor and down the hall, meanwhile, the object of these reveries had arrived in Crossley's office. To his surprise, Porter and Stellworth were there. Crossley was studiously avoiding his eyes.

".The full gathering of the coven," Doberman said.

Crossley cleared his throat solemnly. "I gather that Stellworth has already talked to you about this thing. Porter knows about it, too. The question is, what should we do about it at this point?" Nervously, straightening in his chair, he bared his teeth for a second in a smile of the sort that chimpanzees must have had in mind when they decided, as they apparently have, that a smile is a threatening gesture.

Doberman decided to be proactive. "Why do we have to – "

"All in due course, Bill. Let me sum up. You made a big mistake – "

"I don't know if I agree with that."

"It's pretty hard to deny. So now we have to figure out how to minimize the embarrassment. For the firm."

"What embarrassment for the firm? I just don't – "

Porter suddenly stirred. "It really is, Bill. I'm sorry I let the cat out of the bag, but I thought ..."

Suddenly it struck Doberman, if not quite like a thunderbolt then at least a small epileptic seizure. They weren't talking about his frolic with Gidget after all! And probably none of them but Crossley knew about it. Probably he wasn't going to tell anyone about it, maybe because it made him look ridiculous. This was all just about *Tomcat Industries* after all.

What a pleasant surprise it was to have just *Tomcat Industries* to deal with now. And what a pleasant surprise that it was a pleasant surprise. And what a pleasant surprise that it was a pleasant surprise that it … but enough of that. The point was, this might actually turn out to be pretty easy.

Doberman had been thinking about *Tomcat Industries* every now and then, since he knew that Stellworth had only been squelched temporarily. Over the weekend at the office, his basic idea – the Trojan horse strategy - had crystallized sufficiently for him to whip out a yellow legal pad for a test drive. Like Pythagoras with a theorem, he had gone straight to work.

"1. It's their brief, not ours.

2. Ergo, it's their mistake not ours."

Hence the Trojan horse label. Doberman had left the citation error outside their gates, but they were the fools who had dragged it into their citadel.

"3. I phoned them promptly to report the reversal."

This was the new twist that really had transformed it all for him. It wasn't true, of course, that he had called Nesson & Wesson, but by saying it with enough confidence and circumstantial detail he could turn any dispute with them into a mere swearing contest in front of Barlow. Ashby & Cinders' corporate interests would dictate backing him on this one all the way no matter what.

"4. Phone N & W again A.M. next Thursday 5/12 to confirm."

This was the new twist in support of the new twist. Nesson & Wesson ought to have disseminated a draft reply brief by that time, unless they were disorganized or deliberately dragging their feet. Whether they had or not, however, he could call them to discuss *Tomcat Industries*, and casually refer back to the earlier phantom phone call. With any luck, they would still not have reviewed the cite. It was not really one of their own, and the government had not mentioned it in its opening brief. So perhaps they would think that it didn't need reply brief coverage. If so, then with minimum time to decide how to handle the problem (lest the government attack in its own reply brief), they might be inclined to adopt straight-out confession, albeit perhaps just in a footnote. But he was prepared to do considerably better in his review of their assignment of risk section.

"5. Revise reply brief – show Barlow who are the better lawyers."

Q.E.D. Or perhaps, case, set, and match. The basic idea here was a simple one. No two cases, any more than any two snowflakes, are exactly identical. So, given any Case A and Case B, they will be alike in some respects and different in others. If A comes out right for your position in B, argue the similarities. If it comes out wrong, argue the differences. Doberman was pretty sure that he could make the argument, counter-intuitive though it might be, that the reversal of *Tomcat Industries*, although it meant the manufacturer had lost, actually made Barlow's legal position stronger. The revised precedent showed just how much you need for plaintiffs to prevail on assumption of risk. A differently-named litigant in a different industry, for example.

More specifically, Doberman had a new perspective on the fact that Barlow had put TDC in a new brand of cigarette. He now really felt that this might permit him to make hay out of the winning ground for reversal in *Tomcat Industries* (old users not on notice about the change in a preexisting product). By putting TDC only in the new brands, which consumers ought to know might have different risks than the old ones, hadn't Barlow presciently provided exactly the kind of notice that the court in *Tomcat Industries* was insisting on? On first reading he had dismissed this argument on the ground that the Surgeon General's warning was generic, hence not logically to be read as suggesting that each new cigarette brand might involve a distinct set of risks. Doberman now felt, however, that this argument might be entirely too subtle for the Commission if no one should happen to expressly make it for them.

Hence an additional advantage of the approach Doberman

now favored: it would blindside, or was it wrong-foot or jujitsu, the government reply brief, which, if it didn't miss the reversal altogether, would flag it with a fervor that the revised Barlow reply brief could suggest was entirely misplaced. Nowhere was the government reply brief likely to give sufficient emphasis to the argument in its favor that here, unlike in *Tomcat Industries*, multiple brands should be regarded as effectively the same so far as notice was concerned.

Doberman could have tried to explain all this to his colleagues, although their patience and sympathy might, at least in some quarters, be open to question. Why bother, however? It would be an intelligence blunder all over again. He calmly eyed each of them in turn before speaking.

"Like I said, why do we have to do anything? What mistake? What embarrassment for the firm? I pull off a coup and all I get is flack. You guys are disappointing me. Haven't you ever heard of the Trojan horse strategy?"

"The what?!?" came from all three of them.

"You wouldn't understand. So just don't do anything. I'll handle it."

He rose and left the room, feeling a thrill because he had never walked out on a partner before. Crossley was a lost cause, so there was nothing to be gained by truckling to him anyway.

Crossley found himself trembling from the surprise and the defiance. Bearded in his very office twice, by the same impertinent young varlet! (The actual word choice in his head was somewhat cruder.)

"Okay," he finally said to the other associates. "The meeting's over. You can go. I'll decide how to handle this, all in due course."

Porter stumbled right out, but Stellworth lingered, staring with uncharacteristic assertiveness right into Crossley's eyes. "That individual who necessitated this meeting is *not* partnership material," he said, enunciating even more clearly than usual. "He does *not* do things the Ashby & Cinders way,"

"You can say that again. I guarantee you one thing. He will not be making partner this Friday."

"Thank you. That's really what's right." Stellworth almost offered to shake Crossley's hand, but then thought better of it and awkwardly withdrew.

"But that doesn't mean you should count on making it either," continued Crossley softly once he knew that Stellworth was out of earshot.

17. Many Happy Returns

There are a number of lines of dialogue that you can count on hearing when you watch a Western movie on late night television. One is the banter on the prairie: "It's quiet out here tonight." – "Yep, a little too quiet." Another is the bar scene where the guns are about to come out and someone, perhaps the proprietor, says "I just don't want any trouble."

Doberman could have delivered any of these lines with conviction as the two-week run that would end with Partnership Night trundled slowly forward. It was quiet, a little too quiet, and he just didn't want any trouble.

Crossley was ominously silent. He must have decided not to do anything about the citation error, perhaps on the theory that leaving it glaringly uncorrected would put Doberman in the worst possible position. Perhaps he would even insist on Partnership Night that he had been after Doberman the whole time, unsuccessfully demanding a correction memo. This is how Doberman might have considered handling it in his shoes, although perhaps it required more nerve than Crossley had.

Lyla, Doberman spoke with daily and saw over the

weekend. Things were certainly placid enough, although she was acting oddly reserved. Maybe she just thought that he was too abstracted and preoccupied given the drama of having gotten engaged. At some point he would have to think about this a bit more.

Gidget, he did not see. He avoided the floor that she was working on and stayed out of the elevators at nine and five o'clock. She was evidently staying out of his way, too.

Finally, it was time for the closing sprint. Nesson & Wesson had promised to send over a draft of the Barlow reply brief by no later than noon on Thursday, May 12. Just after 10:30 that morning, knowing that the draft was unlikely to have gone out yet, he called them and asked for the senior-most partner whose name had appeared on the first-stage Barlow brief.

"I'm just calling to follow up on something before you send the draft over," he said after the preliminaries. "Hopefully I didn't need to call, but maybe this will save us all some time. It's about a case called *Tomcat Industries*. You may remember we called you right after sending you our version of the main brief to make sure you knew it had been reversed."

"What case is this?"

"*Tomcat Industries*. Assumption of risk on an over-the-counter diet pill. I spoke to one of your associates, I don't remember who. Maybe Don Peters, but I couldn't swear to it." (From the listing on the brief, Peters was evidently the most junior Nesson & Wesson associate on the case.)

"It's been reversed, you say?"

"Yes. But somehow the cite came out wrong in your submission to the FPHC. The favorable holding that the brief relies on was reversed on rehearing a couple of days before you even filed. You guys should know about this although you seem to have screwed it up the first time around; I just wanted to make sure that you're planning to take care of it now."

"This whole thing is news to me. We'll have to get back to you." Click.

Poor Peters, Doberman thought. Still, we are put on this vale of tears to go through experiences that will make us wiser and stronger. He buzzed his secretary to tell her that, if Peters or anyone else from Nesson & Wesson should call today, she should say he was tied up in meetings and would try to call back later. If they called a second time, she should say that he was definitely tied up until tomorrow.

Peters called back within ten minutes, and then a second time in the early afternoon, but was turned back at the gate each time as per instructions. He did send through a message each time that it was urgent - Doberman should call him back immediately - and that revised reply brief text concerning *Tomcat Industries* would be coming over by Friday morning at the latest. Doberman made a note to himself to return the call on Friday once he saw how they handled it in the revision. The twelve o'clock version had not mentioned it.

The little dance with Peters lifted Doberman's spirits, which had been sagging a bit under the various strains he faced. Tomorrow's partnership meeting was of course front and center - a bit like the Sun in the sky at high noon on Mercury. But there were also a couple of side annoyances - one might say, incoming comets with suspicious trajectories - that he had been pushing aside in his mind (not, alas, in the sky) for too long.

One was the too-quiet Cinders. (Crossley, he just couldn't worry about at this point.) Doberman needed to talk to Cinders before the partnership meeting, but had been hoping the great man would make the first overture. Given the ugly terms on which they had last parted and the subsequent news suggesting that Stellworth had inadvertently mended their fences, Doberman had been hoping for a reconciliation in its own way as passionate, if not quite so physical, as the one he had recently experienced with Lyla. Nothing but silence, however, so, with the zero hour rapidly approaching he apparently would have to make the first move, and with no way of being certain in advance of its favorable reception.

Then there was Lyla. While superficially everything was fine, he knew her well enough to realize that there had been a distinct seismic shift in her affect since the chat when she had mentioned her father. At this stage in the cycle, she simply shouldn't be so chilly and remote. If the bloom was off again, then they should have gone on to the next stage, and she ought to be snapping at him. Instead, she was being icy or even ironic in some unusually subtle way, and yet at the same time extra polite.

Was it just consideration for the strain he was under on Partnership Week? Not more than slightly; that would have a different flavor. Anyway she would not just be sympathizing with him even if nothing else was wrong. The partnership decision was a kind of test that would influence her respect for him. He was supposed to make it if he was the person, and offered the future, that he claimed.

At least Gidget was unlikely to be a problem. Word had it that she had given notice to her bosses and was returning home to southern California. She would probably say a discreet goodbye to him, although this was not entirely certain. He felt strongly, however, that she had accepted the verdict and would not be trying to win him back, or else to convince him of the error of his ways so she could be the one to dump him, or else to berate him before she left, or any of the other permutations that he might in some cases have expected. So at least this comet was likely headed well off to the side, and on the verge of swinging back into deep interstellar space.

Doberman was about to learn, however, that he was no astronomer. A multi-comet collision, rare since the earliest days of the Solar System, was headed right his way.

Lyla arrived first. At lunch she had heard office scuttlebutt, recently transmitted from the secretaries to the paralegals, to the effect that Doberman was in deep doo-doo. What had happened? Unclear, but Cinders was angry at him. When had it happened? Maybe as much as a couple of weeks ago.

Doberman had not so much as hinted at this when he asked her to marry him that night, or even at dinner beforehand when they were discussing his prospects. Nor had he suggested it since. Was this simply because he did not want to seem weak and pitiable? Maybe so, but it would have been nice if he had seemed more genuinely surprised when she told him about her father.

Lyla was merely stopping by in his office to have an exploratory discussion about all this, having learned so recently and keenly about the peril of false, or at least unsupported, accusation. She planned just to ask him directly about what, if anything, had gone on with Cinders, and when it had happened relative to the engagement. If he confirmed the account of a blowup, she could ask why he had not mentioned it before. He should trust her with bad news as well as good. She would not advert to her suspicions about his motives for the wedding engagement unless she could do so dispassionately and with an air of: Look what I'm struggling with; can you help me?

She found him courteous but dismissive. Yes, there had been a spot of disagreement with Cinders at some point recently, whether before or after the engagement he could not quite recall. It was a long story and he could tell it to her it later. But really it was no big deal. This was why he had never mentioned it. Already it had blown over, and they were again good friends. Cinders had left propitiously timed word for him to stop by this afternoon or tomorrow morning.

Things were just winding down to a close, still oddly formal but with no evident disharmony, when Gidget burst into Doberman's office. She was looking flushed and her eyes were red.

"Bill," she said, "I need to talk with you. It's really important." Then, looking at Lyla, "I'm sorry, but I really need two minutes."

Lyla was holding her ground. "I'm his fiancee, you know. Whatever it is, I can hear it, too."

This was the first time she had forgotten her promise to keep the engagement a secret until after the partnership verdict.

"Okay," Gidget said. "I don't know if you really want to hear this, but you're probably entitled."

She turned to Doberman. "Bill," she said, "I'm pregnant. I was starting to wonder about feeling funny, and at lunchtime I went to a clinic and took the test."

Doberman, reeling, knew that there was one question you should never ask when someone tells you this, at least not right away. It might be necessary before finalizing any arrangements, but that was a different matter. You are simply not supposed to greet this news, under any circumstances, with the question, "Am I definitely the father?"

There was a ripe pause.

"Am I definitely the father?" he asked.

Gidget blushed; her code was not so liberal as this seemed to imply. "You're definitely the father. No one else could be."

It was indeed just over a month since their first time together. Doberman recalled that, in the throes and also simulating the throes, he had not used a condom that time, so it checked out. The other times he hadn't used a condom, in New York and then in Crossley's office, seemed a bit too recent; the latter definitely was. But of course you didn't need to supply sperm on the installment plan in order to get someone pregnant.

Lyla, her voice dry ice, cut in. "Gidget, I take it you are telling us that Bill *is* capable of being the father. Biologically, based on what happened between you, I mean."

Gidget could not help smiling. "I'd say there's no doubt about that."

Lyla took a step towards the door. "I'll just leave you two

to work it out. Bill, we'll talk later?" And she left without a look back.

Doberman flinched as if he had been slapped. In fact, he would have greatly preferred being slapped to this. Why couldn't Lyla scream at him, pound the table, shake a fist in his face? All these would have been far better signs, looking down the road a bit, than the way she actually had reacted.

There is a second question that you are not supposed to ask immediately upon getting the news that you have made someone pregnant – at least, not if the prospective mother is Irish Catholic, as Gidget was. The question is: "Are you willing to have an abortion?"

The declarative form is even worse: "We need to have an abortion." And worse still is the more distancing declarative statement: "You need to have an abortion." Worst of all is to immediately add the offer: "I'll pay for it."

Unfortunately for Doberman, however, his gears were still stripped. "You need to have an abortion," he heard himself saying to her. "Of course I'll pay for it."

"No way," said Gidget. This was the first time he had ever seen her angry. But then she started to sniffle. He walked around her to close the office door, on second thought locked it, and then stepped back to her. She accepted his arms around her and cried on his shoulder. Before long she calmed down and pushed him away.

Feeling awkward standing there, he walked back around his desk and sat on his chair. Courteously, he hoped, he tried to motion her into the loveseat. For a second it seemed she would refuse, but then, perhaps not feeling her best, she accepted.

"Bill, I'm not having an abortion. That's final. I know you can be very persuasive, but there's no point this time. I've decided, and I'm not even going to give you the chance."

"Why not? It's totally safe. And I think it would be better for you."

Gidget shook her head. "I've been in this situation once

before. About eight years ago. It was with my high school boyfriend. I decided never to go through it again, no matter what."

"Why not?" Doberman was struggling to regain his self-control. At least this was better than asking "Why the hell not?" or even "Why on earth not?"

"We broke up because of it, but that's not the point. I had nightmares about it for months, and even now I have them occasionally. In my head I have nothing against abortion; I believe in abortion rights. But it's not something I'm willing to do again."

"What are your other choices?" This seemed a tactful way of putting certain pragmatic considerations in front of her.

"I've thought about that. I was already moving back to Coronado. Now I'll just move in with my parents. They'll be okay with this."

"What'll you do?"

"I was thinking I'd become a nursery school teacher. I've always loved kids, especially since it happened. I've done years of babysitting. I think it'll actually be good."

"I suppose you'll want child support."

She shook her head, and Doberman considered drafting a quick contract and asking her to sign it. This might backfire, however, and anyway it probably wouldn't help in court. Too bad. Once she got around to living with her parents and having to buy diapers and baby food on a nursery school teacher's salary, she'd probably want the child support. He really couldn't blame her on that one.

"Are you sure you know what you're getting into?" he asked. "Is this really what you want?"

"I think so. But anyway it's not just me. I have to do this. I'm sorry." She stepped to the door, opened it gingerly, and left before he could say anything further.

Doberman felt certain that there was no point to tracking her down and trying to get her to change her mind. One way or another, he would simply have to accept what had just happened as a fact.

Did he ever want to see the child? Did he even care what sex it was? These were questions for another day.

Lyla was a more immediate concern. She needed to hear as soon as possible that he had slept with Gidget only once, right after the big blowout at the airport (when he had after all threatened to look her up). Did this date, a couple of weeks after the actual likely moment of insemination, leave enough time for a detectable pregnancy? He would just have to hope that it was close enough to pass.

About an hour later – he had spent it daydreaming but was planning to bill the time anyway – Lyla came in and closed the door.

"What do you have to say to me?" she asked.

"I'm sorry."

"No roses this time. You're a pig."

"I'm really sorry. I'm so sorry. But you know, I only slept with her right after our blow-up at the airport. I was so upset I called her that night."

"What time was that? Wasn't it a bit late to call if you weren't already together?" A bit on the skeptical side, but at least she was listening.

"It was, but I told her I had to see her. She agreed right away. It happened pretty fast when I got there, but it didn't feel right afterwards. I realized I was only doing it because I was angry at you. That's why I started sending you roses as soon as I figured there was any chance that you wouldn't just throw them in the trash. I felt bad. Otherwise I definitely wouldn't have done anything so soon. Although I was always planning to at some point."

Lyla seemed to relax just a hair. This part was almost believable.

"But in that case, isn't today a bit early for a pregnancy test?" she finally asked.

"I don't know. I would have thought so, too. But obviously I believe Gidget about it."

Lyla sighed. "I don't know," she said. "I'm going to have to think about this a bit more. I'm also wondering about the Cinders thing again. Did you know about my father and his law firm before I told you? I got the feeling that maybe you did. Is that why you proposed to me?"

Doberman was shocked; one might almost say shocked, shocked.

"That would be horrible," Lyla said. "I would be so humiliated! I'm humiliated already. No matter what I do I'm humiliated."

He was silent so she could finish.

"I don't like being humiliated," she said. "Maybe some of your girlfriends like it, but I don't."

He mumbled something supportive-sounding.

"Here's what I think now," she continued. "If you bomb out here, I'm not helping you get a job at Carp, Stone & Tyler or anywhere else. If you behave, and I really mean behave, then maybe I'll marry you if you make partner here. That's the least I deserve. If after that I ever get even the least whisper of more shenanigans from you, I'll divorce you on the spot. Then you can add alimony to the child support that I'm sure Gidget is asking you for.

"Is all that clear enough?" she asked. He nodded dumbly and she marched out of the room.

18. Hail Mary Pass

Doberman slept like a toddler on Thursday night. That is, he woke up crying from a bad dream and wet the bed.

In the morning, needing inspiration on this of all days, he thought of a quotation from Winston Churchill. How did it go exactly? He got out a Bartlett's that he still had from college, and looked for the words that he needed. No, not the quote about blood, toil, tears, and sweat; that was pretty redundant at this point. Here it was at last:

"We shall not flag or fail. We shall go on to the end. We shall fight in France, we shall fight on the seas and oceans, we shall fight with growing confidence and growing strength in the air, we shall defend our island, whatever the cost may be. We shall fight on the beaches, we shall fight on the landing grounds, we shall fight in the fields and in the streets, we shall fight in the hills; we shall never surrender."

That about said it. He gulped down the last of his coffee and headed for the office.

First things first. A trip to the mailroom landed him a copy of Nesson & Wesson's proposed insertion to the draft reply brief. Sure enough, the reversal of *Tomcat Industries* had been

179

handled a bit awkwardly, plainly showing the consequences of embarrassment and haste. A new paragraph, meant to go in the middle of a discussion of federal regulatory cases, started with the less than stirring declaration: "Nor is the case law concerning private causes of action in tort in any significant respect to the contrary." It then string-cited eight or ten cases from various circuits, their holdings discussed only in brief parentheticals, and closed with a footnote that began: "This conclusion concerning private causes of action in tort follows notwithstanding *Tomcat Industries* ..." The footnote then attempted to distinguish the case through the kitchen-sink method of mentioning everything but explaining nothing.

Doberman had managed by this time to rough out a better approach, which he now finalized and got typed up. Early in the assumption of risk section, where the doctrine was being discussed in more general terms, he proposed to state: "Just how clear the law is on this matter is shown by *Tomcat Industries* ..." He then offered two full paragraphs of main text - no pathetically transparent and ineffectual efforts at concealment via relegation to the footnotes for him! - explaining in detail why the revised decision was even better for Barlow than the original one. It showed just how seriously courts take explicit medical warnings on new products with their own brand names, as opposed to warnings that are merely retained on "New and Improved" versions of existing products.

Substance aside, however, the key was to achieve an undertone of seeming pleased, rather than in any way embarrassed or discomfited, by the turn that the case had taken. Brief-reading judges may retain the art of the schoolyard bully in sniffing out (and also despising) felt vulnerability.

Once this was done, Doberman had his secretary place a call to Don Peters at Nesson & Wesson. The lad sounded glad to hear from him.

"Bill, I've been trying to reach you. That case, *Tomcat Industries*, that the appeals court reversed?"

"Yes. I've just been working on it."

"We sent over some language on it this morning."

"I know."

"But were you saying you called to tell me about the reversal before we filed?"

"It might have been you I spoke to. I'm not sure."

"It definitely wasn't me. We've never spoken before, and I definitely never heard the case had been reversed. I don't know how we missed it, but I know we got the case from your firm's memo."

"Well, I know it got reversed right after we sent you our version, or at least that's when the new Shepard's came in to the library. I always check for new Shepard's if I have a pending matter."

Peters mentally noted this. Maybe from now on he should follow the same practice.

"Anyway," Doberman continued, "I know I spoke to someone. Tell me who else in your shop was working on the case."

There were four names besides Peters and the senior partner. Doberman judiciously weighed each. One, a woman, he ruled out altogether. Two were long shots but possible, and the final one just might be but he wasn't certain.

Or maybe the call had been misdirected by the switchboard operator to someone who wasn't even working on the Barlow case. Then that person might have thought Doberman was calling to discuss something else, and put the whole thing out of mind once he realized it wasn't pertinent. That would be just typical.

"But enough about past mistakes," Doberman finally counseled. "The important thing to avoid any future ones, and focus on what we do next."

Peters was all ears. At his stage he did not get to talk to lawyers at other firms very often.

Despite having baited the hook, Doberman now pulled

in the line. "I can't really tell you right now because we're still working on it. But I think you'll see that we're proposing to handle the reversal a bit more creatively. Good talking to you."

Doberman hung up, thinking: That should hold them. He could now report, for transmission to Barlow Industries, that Nesson & Wesson had more or less conceded its screw-up and was trying to figure out internally what had happened. He buzzed for his secretary, and when she came in instructed her to send his paragraphs on *Tomcat Industries* to everyone - the client and Nesson & Wesson as well as the Barlow team at Ashby & Cinders - without waiting for Crossley to review it and clear its dissemination first.

It was time now for the Hail Mary pass – the long strike to snatch victory from the slobbering jaws of defeat. Let Crossley hate me, he thought, and, yes, even resent and envy me, all that he likes. I'd put up even money now with Cinders at the bat.

For a couple of weeks now he and Cinders had not met, and their last meeting had ended in sorrow, Doberman's at any rate. But perhaps not only; Doberman sometimes thought he could discern a spark of – Appreciation? Recognition? This young man is just like I used to be? Or refreshingly not like I ever was? It didn't really matter which.

As he girded for the as yet unscheduled reunion, Doberman thought of Romeo and Juliet – Pyramis and Thisbe – Ryan O'Neal and Ali – hopefully, not Ali and Frazier.

Like a Hollywood screenwriter laying his plans for a meeting with a movie executive, he needed both a pitch and a slightly lengthier treatment. The question to be answered was: Why exactly should Cinders concern himself with a mere miserable ant whose life was up for bid at the partnership meeting that night?

Pretty soon he had it. Now the only problem was getting in to see Cinders on such short notice. He wheedled the great man's secretary a bit, and she agreed to squeeze him in at 3:45

sharp and to hold non-essential calls if Cinders assented. The partnership meeting was set for 6 o'clock.

Cinders' greeting when Doberman was at last invited into his office – not all that late, really, at five minutes to four – was reasonably cordial though perhaps a bit opaque.

"Mr. Cinders," Doberman started, "I wanted to alert you to a problem that may become a concern. Or rather, I have a concern and I hope that it doesn't become a problem."

Cinders gazed back blankly as if to say, Yes, but what does that matter to me?

"It's about some of the junior partners' viewpoints – I don't want to name any names – about the criteria for excellence here."

Cinders looked perhaps a hair more interested, but still not much.

Doberman kept trying. "Not everyone here shares your interpretation, and the one I learned from you, of our priorities here."

"Meaning?"

"Well, partly it's billable hours versus the rest. I'm up for partnership today, as I guess you know, and I'd say my billables are pretty irreproachable. About twenty-four hundred over the last year. But the question is, is that all I bring to the table that's relevant?"

"Partnership is not just about the hours you bill. It's the value you bring."

"I know that. That's my point. But I don't just mean credit for everything I did in those twenty-four hundred hours – I think I'm the best young lawyer here, but that's not for me to say. I also mean, what are the other things that count?"

"Get to the point."

"Okay. Crossley says that the peripherals, like culture and good works and charitable boards and broader contacts, don't matter at all. He says you're wrong about that. Soft-headed is the word I think he used."

"What!?" Cinders found this hard to believe, but for Pavlovian reasons it had the desired effect anyway. It was distressing that Crossley could even be associated with such ugliness.

"Of course, he'll deny it if you say I told you about it. He's pretty much told me that. But he also said it's time for new blood to be making more of the firm's decisions.

"Anyway, he thinks that when my name comes up at the meeting tonight, I shouldn't get any of the credit for the things I do outside of the twenty-four hundred hours. If anything, he thinks it should be a demerit.

"Maybe you don't fully believe me. But you will when he starts speaking up against you at the meeting tonight. He says he's willing to do that, if that's what it takes."

Cinders spoke at last. "Thanks for the tip. I'll certainly keep my eyes and ears open."

He looked ready to end the meeting, but this still wasn't good enough. Doberman pressed on.

"Two more things. One, again I'm really sorry about the opera. But I didn't tell you the real reason I wasn't able to go. The fact is, Crossley wouldn't let me. He basically made me stay in the office on the night of the performance."

"Why didn't you say that before? I seem to recall something about a medical problem."

"I was covering for him. But at this point I really don't see why I should."

"You said you had two more things."

"Yes. The second is that I really think you need me in that kind of slot, like for opera and such. No one else on the horizon here can do it."

Cinders didn't contradict this. He seemed to be thinking about it.

"Can I still be frank?" Doberman asked.

"Go ahead."

"I'm not sure if Stellworth really screwed up the opera, or if it was a kind of Trojan horse strategy."

"What do you mean?"

"A deliberate wrong tip. Leave it out on the plain, as it were, so that I and then you would drag it into the citadel, so to speak. Leaving me with the blame."

"That doesn't make sense," Cinders objected. "He admitted to me that he was the one at the opera."

"Did he? That's interesting; I wouldn't have guessed. Well, I'd have to agree that gets him off the hook on the Trojan horse strategy, but maybe it's even worse. Like you were saying before, that means he honestly couldn't tell the difference between Luga and an understudy."

"He's also not too strong on the contemporary art scene. You should have seen him the other day when I took him to an opening." Cinders seemed to shudder at the recollection.

Doberman was dying to hear the details, but realized he couldn't indulge himself now. He had more important rats to fry.

"All this is just a long-winded way of saying, I hope you'll support me at the partnership meeting tonight. A week ago, even a couple of days ago, I would have thought it wasn't necessary. I mean, specially asking you wouldn't be necessary. I know of course that I would need your support. But while I've known all along that Crossley is against me, probably because he's jealous of some things, until now I figured he didn't have anything on me, and pretty much would have to accept the consensus.

"But now I'm starting to be afraid that he does think he has something on me. Ironically, it's because I did something right – not a mistake like he's going to say it is."

Cinders gave him a sharp glance. "So, at last we get to the point."

"Are you familiar with some recent developments in our representing Barlow Industries?"

"They're my client. We've been getting some new business from them lately, and more may be about to follow."

"I'm on brief in the FPHC case."

"I know all about it."

Hopefully not quite all, Doberman was thinking. "Anyway, I took assumption of risk in our crack at the first-stage brief because it was the most important topic. I cited a case when I wrote it up on a Friday, actually make that Sunday but there's no mail delivery in the library over the weekend. Then the next Tuesday we get the new Shepard's – the red pamphlet you know – " (Cinders tried to look as if he remembered) "- and it turned out the circuit court just issued a new opinion reversing everything they said before in the case I cited on Sunday."

"Had you thought of trying Lexis?" It was surprising that Cinders had heard of this still fairly new electronic citation service.

"They're always a few days behind, too. Anyway, I could have tried to pull back our brief, but then we would have looked really bad. We couldn't have re-typed it all in time without making a mess. To make a long story short, I called Nesson & Wesson, the other firm in the case, to give them the heads-up about the reversal, but they screwed it up, they're still trying to figure out how. So the brief was filed with an error, and now at Nesson they're being really dopey and almost mea culpa in the reply brief, and I've come up with a great way to handle it, almost like it was a Trojan horse strategy, but Crossley won't listen to me. So I sent it out anyway without his approval, which you know I normally wouldn't do.

"He wants us to take the mea culpa route. He insists it's because I screwed up, but, if he really wants to make me the fall guy, the price is simple: we lose the client, at least on litigation and administrative matters. I have it perfectly set up so Nesson & Wesson gets the blame and we get the credit, but Crossley may not think it's worth it if 'we' includes me."

"And?"

"I'm telling you this in case it comes up at the partnership meeting. So you can defend me on it. It's exactly the same line we can take with Barlow when they get around to reviewing the play by play on the reply brief."

Doberman paused to take a deep breath. "Also, if I'm the fall guy then I might just take it up with Barlow myself. Explain to them how I perceive things happened, and which things I'm responsible for and which not. Maybe they'll be interested in where I'm going if I don't make it here. Not that I expect that."

"And where would that be?"

"I'd rather not say. Ashby & Cinders is where I want to be."

Cinders rather liked this shift to truculence and something bordering on softcore blackmail. It suggested that Doberman had some backbone.

"You're quite right, by the way," he said, "that Barlow is emerging as a more significant client. My impression is the same as yours, that they've liked our work on the FPHC matter. There's been talk of another matter, not an insubstantial one but really more important as a harbinger. An oil pipeline case in Alaska. If we get that one and do a good job on it, a lot of other things may follow as well.

"Okay, I've heard enough. I'll think about it."

"You know, I'll really owe you a debt if I make it. If you want to say you own me, I won't complain."

"I'll definitely remember that."

"Can I hope that you'll support me?"

"I'll do my best. But you know I'm not a dictator here."

The meeting was over, and Doberman left.

Heading back to his office, he tried to weigh Cinders' final words as precisely as he could. They were not entirely meaningless, since they could so easily have been chillier or at least blander. Still, they could mean anything from, "It's in the bag but I always give my standard disclaimer," to "Good try, kid. It didn't really work, but I liked it enough to be nice to you afterwards by telling you I gave it my best shot."

19. Night of the Long Knives

As the ancient Greeks had the Mysteries of Eleusis, so Ashby & Cinders had its annual partnership meeting. Each was open only to the few elect who had been chosen and initiated, and who were bound in honor to the secrecy of their order. Each had its high priests and celebrants, as well as its trembling initiates awaiting the summons that would symbolize the passage from death and dross to a kind of eternal life.

Let us eavesdrop now on the poets who have sought in all ignorance to imagine that which they could never personally know. "Soon the thunder rolled and lightning flashed," goes a typical account of the older Mysteries that could stand for either, "while strange and fearful objects appeared. The place seemed to shake and be on fire; hideous specters glided through the building, moaning and sighing; frightful noises and howlings were heard. Then, wheeling and circling against the sky, came mysterious apparitions, representing the messengers of the infernal deities, Anguish, Madness, Famine, Disease, and Death."

Differences there were, to be sure. At Eleusis there may

have been psychedelic mushrooms, along with snake dances and apparently the ritual slaughter by initiates of a pig. At Ashby & Cinders there was only Chinese takeout food in the large conference room, while the slaughter, in contrast, was *of* the initiates and – if one adopts the 1960s lingo that a few of the senior associates still dimly remembered - *by* the pigs.

Also, one imagines that at Eleusis things built steadily to a deafening climax during the course of the revels. At Ashby & Cinders, the loudest cries usually came early in the proceedings, when the partners were settling the really important question of how the year's profits should be divided. Though none of them was hurting financially by the standards most people would apply, greed and ego tended to mix a potent cocktail. Relative calm typically prevailed during the later stages when mere desiderata, such as the site for next year's annual retreat or the fate of some poor associate who was hoping to make partner, came up for consideration.

Partnership night this time around was a little different, however. Heated voices could be heard at times even towards the end, although only by the secretaries on late duty sitting just outside. Everyone else, no matter how curious, was staying far away.

Throughout the firm's offices, one could see that this was a special evening. Partnership row was even more deserted than would be usual at the approach of the weekend. The library had nearly its full complement of Friday night associates, but generally with three notable exceptions. Among those present, there was the kind of hush one might expect from a troop of red colebus monkeys when predatory chimps have just killed one of their high-ranking members.

In three smallish offices, senior associates were sitting and waiting for the news, although Doberman from time to time dashed into the library just to show that he was uncowed. He also tried to hunt down the Barlow and government reply briefs, which had been due at the FPHC at 5 o'clock, but apparently Crossley had the only as yet available copies in the office. At ten-thirty, the wait was still ongoing, clear evidence that the partners might be struggling with something unusually contentious.

Finally the meeting broke up. Most of the partners headed rapidly for the elevators without speaking in the open hallway. Crossley, however, as Associates Liaison on the Hiring and Promotion Committee, had three visits to make before he could leave for the night.

Porter, the first visitee, had his door closed and was trying to read a Dickens novel. This had been Janet's idea to relax him, but he could not focus. He had actually been staying pretty calm all week, but once he left for home on Thursday night the stoic feeling had deserted him.

Last night, even Brian and Ted had seemed to notice the gloom and tension in the household. Maybe that was why they had kept watching videos instead of trying to get him to play. Then each boy had insisted that Mom read him a story first, leading to a squabble that Porter had let Janet handle entirely by herself, figuring that he wouldn't be in good form anyway.

Porter felt as if he were on death row, awaiting execution at midnight but tormented by the hope, faint and fading yet just strong enough to prevent him from groping towards acceptance, that the Governor might call to reprieve him. He kept ruminating about Louis XVI, who apparently did not die at the very instant he was guillotined, since reportedly his eyes, as his head was held up to the crowd, blinked and looked around for several seconds.

At long last Porter heard two short knocks on his door and Crossley entered, dressed in the black suit that he evidently thought was in the proper spirit for the occasion. Crossley looked very tired, an omen that was hard to interpret.

After not much in the way of preliminaries, Crossley got down to business.

"Arnold, you know tonight was the annual partnership meeting."

Porter nodded wordlessly.

"We had a full discussion of your candidacy for partnership. You've had six good years here, we all appreciate what you've done, and we gave a very fair consideration of where we go from here."

This sounded pretty bad. At least he hadn't said the discussion was frank or candid.

"I have to say there was a real consensus here on some of the main elements. We feel you've done a lot of good work. You're a solid lawyer. Not much spark. A bit shy with clients. Some of us had questions about initiative and leadership ability."

Here it came.

"We don't feel you're partnership material at the firm under current circumstances."

Porter gave the blink and swallow that Crossley, over the years, had come to know so well. He was not finished, however.

"And that's why we've decided, well, to offer you an of-counsel position here. You can keep your current salary and duties. Legal research and memos; you know the drill pretty well. You may, by the way, get to write the Barlow brief if we end up in district court, as I suspect we will. Of course, that depends on whether they give us the brief. But anyway, it will be that type of that thing, like you're used to.

"I should probably say a bit more. Small annual raises based on merit are possible, but we won't be considering you for partner again. At least, not under current circumstances. You can think of the position as effectively indefinite, but without the creation of any long-term rights or expectations. Next week or at your convenience, we can discuss a possible one or two-year contract with the firm."

Porter ran a hand over his eyes. So the Governor had called after all. If not a full pardon, at least it sounded a bit like commutation to a life sentence. Would the offer, if he accepted it (and he suspected he would), brand him as a permanent loser and target of ill-hidden scorn in the firm's hallways? Or would it mark him as a survivor, and one now as far beyond the ordinary passions as a eunuch amid the Emperor's harem?

Porter felt too dazed to really think it through now. He had heard somewhere about this type of deal being offered by New York firms to senior associates. But he could not recall its being used this way in Washington, where of-counsels tended to be senior lawyers, perhaps newly retired from the government, who had a valuable specialty but only limited clients or clout. Certainly, it was new at Ashby & Cinders. Things must be changing somehow, on a larger scale than he could appreciate at the moment.

Janet would be glad, anyway. The pride part didn't really matter to her so much as avoiding disruptions, and for that matter continuing to have a decent family income.

Crossley offered him a last grin and a handshake and headed off to his second stop, chez Stellworth. This would possibly be a more ticklish visit.

Stellworth had his door open. While shy of the library, he had decided to spend the evening proofing documents, including some he would ordinarily have farmed out to more junior associates. This was his second straight night at it. Last night he had gotten home after midnight so Sarah would be asleep, although normally he tried to see her each night if work pressures permitted.

With typos already slain in a first run-through, Stellworth was by now concentrating on grammar. He found himself demanding an even higher standard than usual, although few at any time would have considered him lax. Never before in six long years had it occurred to him how boring proofreading can be.

Crossley tapped on the door and entered, offering a deep sigh. He was avoiding Stellworth's eyes, not much of a tip-off since he might be equally uncomfortable sharing good news or bad.

"Lowell," he said, "I have some news for you. It's what you've been waiting for but, well, maybe, not what you've been waiting for."

That did it. Stellworth gave the blink and swallow, actually a kind of audible gulp.

"I don't like telling you this news. It was a tough case, and it really divided the partnership. I fought for you. In fact, I really laid it on the line."

Liar, Stellworth thought, reading something in Crossley's tone. Fool, he thought next, turning his scorn on himself for a change. For some reason, he had really expected Crossley to fight for him. Maybe Cinders had been opposed after the Mapplethorpe disaster, and Crossley had simply been too craven to offer any defense. Assuming that he actually had planned to do so otherwise.

"May I ask what this is based on? Where exactly did I fall short in the estimate of the partners?"

"You didn't fall short at all. It just came down to economics and our reading of the business. In a different year you would have made it for sure.

"We think you are partnership material, but it's not going to be here. Even though you had a lot of support, or maybe because you did, I don't think anyone's going to want to revisit it. You can stay for now, and we will be happy to help in trying to place you. I know you'll land on your feet."

Stellworth gulped again, and his eyes teared over for the first time in more than twenty years. He wanted to ask if Porter or Doberman had made it, but was afraid to. He was going to have to sit down soon and think about what he wanted to do now. Maybe just a second-tier Washington firm, since something was bound to turn up if he really had strong in-house support, but maybe something a lot different.

Return to Boston? Business? Government? Something

outside of law? Although he would never have thought to put it this way, the rising surge of anger, shame, and denial resembled what he might have felt if, on his way home from work the night before, a stranger had overpowered and raped him.

How was he going to tell Sarah? When would he be able to bear to tell his parents?

"Good luck," said Crossley with a nervous grin. "Please tell me when you know what you want to do. Or if there's any way that I can help, or even if you want to talk about it some more." (God forbid.) And he was off to his final stop.

This would be the hardest of all. Crossley's feet dragged as he headed down the hall. How would Doberman react to what he had to say? Would it lead to a scuffle?

Crossley peeked in to see Doberman sitting with pen suspended over pad, evidently absorbed in something.

"Ah, come in, Peter," the words came graciously, although perhaps with less insouciance than intended.

Crossley stepped deliberately through the door and sat on the famous Doberman love seat. It was a little low compared to Doberman's desk chair. He thought of standing up again, but at this point it might look too awkward.

"Bill, I have some news for you. Also some advice. Let me start with the news."

Doberman could feel an adrenaline surge, prompting the fight-or-flight impulse that for the moment he must simply ignore.

"Let me start by saying that your candidacy for promotion was a very divisive issue for the partnership. There was real disagreement about it. It wasn't good for the firm."

"And?"

"I must tell you that I had to be pretty frank about some things. You might not have liked everything that I had to say, or that some others said. But I don't think you could really have contradicted any of it."

"And?"

"Others gave their views, which were not in all cases the same as mine. For a while it was not clear that we would be able to agree on this matter. Although I think we knew that we must and we would."

"So?"

"Purely in the interest of peace, some of us agreed to recede in our views at this point."

Doberman started to smile and pump his right fist.

The next words came out of Crossley's mouth almost as if they were not his but a case of alien possession. "You made it. I can't say I approve, but you made it. Now for the advice."

Doberman gave a whoop, though just a quiet one, and pumped both fists. After a moment Crossley resumed.

"Despite today's result, I would advise you to look elsewhere. Now that you've been promoted it will be a lot easier for you to leave. You can say it's voluntary. But there is still a lot of opposition to you in the partnership, and over time I think it's going to dog you."

"Opposition among my colleagues, you mean. That's not a problem. I'll work on it. We'll all work on it."

"I don't think it's going to be as easy as that."

"Why wouldn't it be?"

"Some of the things I had to say may last a bit. They made an impression even if a very senior partner carried the day."

Good old Cinders! Doberman thought. Then, seeing as they were all partners here, he said it out loud. "Good old Cinders."

"Okay. But good old Cinders is not going to affect your assignments as a junior partner unless he has something to give you. And good old Cinders is not going fight for your financial draw, or to include you in things, or to get you good committee assignments or a nicer office. He generally has better things to do."

Doberman, though still smirking, realized that this was true. "Just what did you tell them?" he asked.

"Just some things I've observed in the last six years and especially the last few weeks."

"Like what? The Barlow brief? My Trojan horse strategy?"

"There were differing views on that. I certainly gave mine."

"Did my language on *Tomcat Industries* end up getting used?"

"Yes. I gave you full credit for that. Although you did it outside channels and of course screwed up the first time around."

"And the government reply brief? Did they miss the boat?"

"You could say so. But I also shared some broader concerns, and where it was useful I provided illustrations."

Doberman felt a twinge of dismay. Even as a newly minted partner he did not want Lyla to get wind of his office encounter with Gidget, as well she might if it had entered general circulation. Even from a position of greater strength, he did not want her back on the warpath.

"Peter. Surely you didn't mention that absurd misunderstanding in your office last week. The one with the secretary I was giving dictation. Miss O'Malley, I think it was."

Crossley actually hadn't brought this up, calculating that the ratio of sniggering at his expense to harm to Doberman would be too unfavorable. Who knew, maybe it would even have boosted Doberman's standing in the partnership. It was still essentially an old boys' club, despite a handful of female partners. (This was before the era of sexual harassment suits, at a time when law firms thought nothing of, say, staging wet T-shirt contests amongst the female summer associates.)

Why set Doberman at ease about the story, however? He would not have asked unless he cared about whether it was disseminated. And it was against Crossley's principles to deny the accusation, no matter how false, of having performed some petty or vindictive deed.

"Bill, I don't think I can answer that question, or really any others about the discussions tonight. Partnership meetings are confidential, you know."

"That didn't seem to be bothering you before."

"Okay. Since you insist. I can't deny the possibility that I may have discussed the matter you bring up."

"I hope you didn't. For your sake. I'll sue you. It's defamation."

Was this really wise of Doberman to say? He wasn't certain. The problem was, his adrenaline was starting to drive him. After all the excitement he was starting to have difficulty controlling himself.

Crossley almost hooted. "Since when can you be sued for defamation for saying something that's true?"

"It's true if you can prove that it's true. Gidget will deny it and so will I."

Doberman did not really know if she would deny it if things came to that, but this was all a bluff anyway. Observing that Crossley seemed unmoved, however, he decided to change gears.

"Now that you've made it public knowledge, just wait until the guys in the mailroom hear about what you say happened. They'll think it's a riot. 'Mr. Crossley, can I have the keys to your office? Or is it already signed up for the night?' 'Mr. Crossley, could you recommend a good rug cleaner?'"

Crossley was shaking his head, but Doberman pressed on.

"They won't say it to your face, of course, but that doesn't mean they won't say it. You'll just see them leering and smirking when you ask for a messenger."

Crossley was starting to get fed up. He had already had a long evening. Getting shorted a bit, as he saw it, on the partnership draw had been a bitter blow. Having Cinders tell him that he lacked good judgment, and was lucky Doberman had bailed him out in the Barlow case, had then made it worse.

By comparison, this dialogue was more like having an itch or a runny nose than anything that really mattered. Still, it was vexing to think that Doberman might always be here – he seemed unimpressed by the advice to seek another firm – safely ensconced as a virtual peer who need not show respect and could respond to any injury by playing tit for tat.

Crossley was tired of all the disrespect at this place, and, come to think of it, at a lot of other places, too. For the last few days, he had been mulling over an interesting opportunity, the fruit of the Hankins dinner, which had paid off better and more swiftly than even Anne had expected. This opportunity really shed new light on what he could hope for so far as status was concerned. Impulsively, he decided to take the leap, a decision he had been leaning towards anyway if the partnership draw and other indications of his internal status should prove disappointing. And why not mention it now? Doberman would be pulled up short, and maybe calculate that he needed to show some deference after all, starting immediately.

Crossley stood up. "Bill, I don't think you'll be seeing too much of me around the mailroom for the next couple of years. I happen to have better plans. You might as well hear about it, although I haven't announced it officially yet."

"Oh?"

"I've recently received a very flattering offer from someone close to the Mondale campaign. Deputy Associate Counsel to the Democratic National Committee. I'm pretty sure I'll be accepting it. And you know what that means."

If Doberman knew, he wasn't saying.

"It could mean Deputy Assistant Associate Attorney General in the Mondale Administration. Or maybe even Assistant Associate Attorney General. And that's just starting out.

"So maybe you should act a bit nicer even if you did make partner tonight over my objections. You might be glad you did, if you ever have to come and ask me for something down the road. The AG's office has a lot of discretion on things.

"One more thing. If I were you I'd still consider the advice I gave you about looking for another firm. I could be back here in a few years with extra clout, you know."

It wasn't a great exit line, but it was the best Crossley had available, so he took it.

Doberman pumped his right fist again as Crossley headed down the hall. That bastard was leaving for the Mondale campaign! This meant the fabled corner office with the view that looked like Paris would actually be available now! Maybe he could get his hands on it somehow. He would have to ask Cinders.

Crossley, meanwhile, was thinking as he headed down the hall: It's interesting that Doberman was so sensitive about that thing with Ms. O'Malley. Maybe I can do him a last little service before I go. Maybe I should make sure his girlfriend finds out about it – that paralegal, Lyla Stamper.

20. The Fruits of Victory

The moment Doberman got home on Friday night, he called Lyla to blurt out the news about his making partner.

"I'm glad for you," she said, not sounding very excited.

"Do you want to celebrate?"

"Not right now. I'm still thinking things over. I need a little time."

"So now you know I didn't propose because of your father."

"I guess."

"Lyla, aren't you – isn't this – "

"It's great. Yes. I know. Why don't we just agree to talk on Monday."

"Lyla. Are we still engaged? Aren't we – "

"I think we are. But I'm really not sure. I'll talk to you Monday."

This pained Doberman more than he would have predicted. Had she insisted that they were still engaged, he might conceivably have resented and regretted it, although he had not yet given much thought to weaseling out. Yet, if there was any chance of her dumping him, he wanted to fight for them to stay together.

He spent a quiet weekend at home, wishing he had someone else to share the news with – someone who cared about him, and could appreciate the feats of daring generalship that had culminated in victory, as much and as unconditionally as he himself did. Even on Monday, he stayed home until almost noon, partly feeling let down and run down, partly because now, at least for the moment, he could. He arrived to learn that the office was buzzing with his two great triumphs: he had made partner, and he and Lyla were engaged to be married. She had decided to announce this to the world without further consulting him first. Perhaps she had feared that he was ready, if she gave him the chance, to call off the engagement before she could publicize it.

"You sly dog!" one of the senior partners who had scarcely ever talked to him before put it, nudging him in the ribs. "You've won the daily double!"

Lyla was not in her office when he tried to call her. She had just had a very interesting conversation with Peter Crossley, who had stopped by to see her after hearing about the engagement. Unbeknownst to Doberman, at the very moment he called her, she was heading over to chat with him in person.

He decided to go see Cinders – luckily enough, as he could tell at a glance upon almost running into Lyla in the hall.

"I just called you," he said, "but at the moment I have to run. Talk to you in a few minutes?"

"You bet. I'll be waiting in your office."

Cinders' secretary ushered him in immediately. Again he heard the golden words, so rare until recent visits, that she should hold all of Cinders' calls unless they were urgent.

"Cedric," he said – the familiar form should certainly be all right now, and he wanted to get used to saying it – "I just wanted to thank you. I don't know how I can, I mean thank you enough, but I'm really grateful."

Cinders simply nodded at receiving his just due.

"I – well, anyway, that's basically it. That's what I wanted to say."

"Is there anything else?"

Did Cinders want still more groveling? Doberman would be happy to oblige, but that did not quite seem to be it. Maybe Cinders actually was willing to just keep on doing favors.

"Well, actually, there is one thing. Has Peter Crossley said anything about his plans?"

"As a matter of fact, he has. He announced something in this morning. I was just going to bring it up myself, but go ahead."

A little breathlessly, Doberman told Cinders how much he had always liked Crossley's office. Was there any way Cinders could help? Assigning offices wasn't really his line, and besides the general rule was that the most senior partner who wanted it would get it, but maybe Cinders could suggest to the office manager that, once Crossley had left, a deadline be set to fill it up fast. That way, maybe Doberman would have a chance.

Cinders frowned. "I don't think that would be a good idea. You'll probably be a bit busy around then – I'll get to that in a second – and I don't want to take the risk that you'll be distracted."

"If I don't get it now, someone else is bound to grab it."

"I know. But can we turn now to the things that I wanted to discuss about Crossley's departure?"

"Of course."

"I have an important suggestion to make. I want you to take this seriously. At the partnership meeting last Friday I got the distinct impression that Crossley doesn't like you very much. Or at least for the moment he's angry at you.

"That's not a good state of affairs. We want him to be on good terms with Ashby & Cinders. In case you didn't hear where he's going, it's to the Mondale campaign. I have sources, and they tell me that in next year's Presidential election

Mondale is probably going to win. Reagan just can't survive the economy, which is likely to get worse before it gets much better. Unless another couple of guys shoot him on television, which seems unlikely. That puts Crossley in the Department of Justice or maybe even the White House. People like that we want to be friends with. Also, when it's time we may want him to think favorably about the possibility coming back. He could be a much bigger asset down the road than he's ever been to this point."

Doberman nodded.

"Anyway," Cinders continued, "you may get a fair portion of his docket when he heads out. So for the next two months, while he finalizes his affairs, I want you to work closely with him. And remember that he's in charge! You're still officially an associate until the end of the calendar year, and besides remember we want him to feel good."

Another nod from Doberman. Was that everything?

"Sit down. I still have a few more things to mention. You did a good job on the Barlow matter. We'll be getting more work with them. With Crossley leaving, some portions of this work will be yours. First thing, in about two months you'll be heading to Alaska."

"Yes, I think you told me about that case."

"Oil pipeline discharge. Administrative litigation. Right up your alley. You'll be spending a couple of weeks there."

"Yes, I see."

"And I'd get a nice warm parka if I were you. There's also talk of Barlow doing a joint oil pipeline venture with the Soviets, in western Siberia. They may want an American lawyer to spend a few weeks there as they negotiate the arrangements and work on the documents. I've been telling them we're jacks of all trades. Probably in December. You'll be in Irkutsk."

Cinders chuckled. "For your information, and I know because I asked, the average daily high in Irkutsk in December is about ten degrees Fahrenheit. I didn't ask about the average daily low. I also didn't ask about the food."

Doberman couldn't quite bring himself to say anything.

"Don't look so dour! You yourself told me how grateful you were, and how if you made partner I'd own you or something.

"Oh, and one last thing. Let's be quite straight about the fact that Barlow is my client. You're just servicing them on my behalf. Crossley almost forgot about this the other day until I reminded him."

That was all. Doberman dazedly trudged back to his office, where Lyla was waiting for him. She still looked angry.

"There's something I need to talk to you about," she said, and for the next few minutes there was just a din of sound coming from her. He couldn't really follow it closely in his current state of mind, even as he kept bleating out apologies and denials. The gist of it was, she still was marrying him but from now on he'd *really* better shape up and fly right or he'd be sorry.

Irkutsk in December, he said to himself. You know something, that doesn't sound half bad.